I'll Make Her Mine

Alpha Gets What Alpha Wants Series, Volume 1

Tennille Stephens

Published by Tennille Stephens, 2023.

This is a work of fiction. Similarities to real people, places, or events are entirely coincidental.

I'LL MAKE HER MINE

First edition. September 1, 2023.

Written by Tennille Stephens.

Table of Contents

Chapter 1

Annabeth
    I watch the scenery out the window of the car, it's almost a full moon outside, and the darkness of the night makes it a beautiful sight. Unfortunately, the euphoria of the night ends there when my mother opens her mouth. "I think you'll fit right in with everyone darling." I roll my eyes, doing my best to ignore her. "I know I messed up for the last sixteen years, but this is a new start." I can feel her eyes on me as she talks.

    "Are you listening to your mother?" The parasite from the driver's side speaks up. I hate this man, he's sleazy and I get a very bad vibe from him. However, my mother married him just last week, making him my new stepfather. I have to bite my tongue, so I don't speak the vile words that wish to come up.

    "Yes, Mother I heard you," I say in an aggravated tone. I can feel the vile man's eyes on me, turning my head a little I see him glaring at me in the mirror. "You didn't mess up Mother. You have always done the best you can." I say in a sugary sweet voice. It does the trick at appeasing her, a bright smile forms on her face, as she beams at me. "Oh darling, this is a fresh start for both of us." She turns back around to face forward, as I hear her deep intake of breath. "We will live like princesses from this day forward." The happiness oozes from her lips.

    The way this woman thinks is appalling to me. I feel we have had a great life. My mother has always been there for me, spent as much time with me as she could, making some clothes for me just the way I like, and showing me love every day. She worked as a waitress since I can remember, living in the same two-bedroom apartment my entire life. Of course, when Arthur came into the picture only three months ago, that all drastically changed.

    Apparently, his car broke down in our small town, so he had to stay at the motel for three days while the town mechanic worked on it. He came into the diner every day, flirting it up with my mom, and showing her a good time. After his car was fixed, he came in to ask for her number. For the next eight weeks, he wined and dined her, giving her a good time. Showing her how the rich and powerful live. Something she has always wanted.

Two weeks ago, he popped the big question, and without a second thought, she accepted. I wasn't even there when they did it. A whirlwind moment she said, whatever the heck that means. She came home in the middle of the night, showing me the ring on her hand. When tears built in my eyes, she looked at me like I was crazy for feeling so sad. Claimed I ruined her special day, as she ran into her bedroom and slammed the door.

Leaving me alone with the creep she married. Don't misunderstand me, Arthur is a good-looking man, he's in his mid-thirties, built like a brick wall, I'm talking muscles for days. He has dark blonde hair and blue eyes. I mean you look at him and you would think he's a girl's wet dream come true. For some reason, which makes me feel crazy, when I look at him, I see the devil with a tail. There's an undertone of danger in how he carries himself.

Not the addicting, hot bad boy danger either. More like there is a sadistic monster within him, and it scares the crap out of me. I try not to let it show, but I swear he can smell my fear. Whenever he's in the same room as me, he lifts his nose, smells the air, and practically licks his lips. Looking at me as though he'd like to eat me up and spit my bones out. I shudder at the thought.

"Annabeth, are you listening to me?" I shake my head at my mother's words. "I'm sorry Mom, I must have dozed off for a minute." She turns her body to face me once more with an incredulous look on her face. "Hello, do you see where we are?" She holds out her hands for emphasis her tone filled with excitement. Looking out the window, I see we are making our way up a long, winding driveway. I can see brick houses as we pass. I feel flabbergasted, "These all belong to this family we are about to meet?" I cannot believe how much land is on their property.

"Yes, everyone that is part of the church lives in those houses." His words make it feel like there's a pit in my stomach. I wasn't raised religiously, and my mother has always been an atheist. I look at the side of her face, and she looks away from me quickly. *What did you do Leslie Ann? Why did you marry this man?* I want to say the words out loud, but I bite the side of my cheek, trying to keep the words at bay.

We finally make it to the end of the driveway, it circles around a grand fountain, and when we park, my mouth falls open. Their house if that is what you can call it is massive. There has to be at least fifteen bedrooms in the house I'm looking at alone. An older man, wearing all black with a top hat and white gloves, opens my mother's door and helps her out of the car. Once Arthur makes his way to her side, he aggressively takes her hand from the older man.

I open my door and go to step out when a hand with long fingers is open palm side up waiting for me to place my hand in his. Looking up, I can see his arm is bigger than one of my legs, his chest is packed, and when my eyes make their way to his face, I'm sitting there stunned. The man looks to be around my age, he has blonde hair cut short, deep brown eyes, and plump beautiful lips. For some reason, I can picture myself biting that bottom lip of his.

"Hi," I squeak out. Clearing my throat, I try once more. "Thank you, but I can get out on my own." I try to keep my voice polite, but when he doesn't move an inch, I can't help but get a little aggravated. "I promise you I can get up by myself." His lips twitch at my snarky tone. I can see he is trying not to smirk at my attitude.

"Oh darling, don't be rude. Allow this handsome, young man to help you out of the car." My mother's voice purrs with flirtation. I expected Arthur to reprimand her, but to my utter shock, he just stands there staring. Although, I can see the tension in his body, and the anger held deep in his eyes.

There must be something with this guy standing in front of me, that makes him keep his mouth shut. That knowledge alone, has me reaching for the beautiful stranger's hand. He lifts me up, with little effort, and so fast I fall into his chest. "Sorry don't know my own strength sometimes." His voice does crazy things to my insides. "I'm Tiberius, but you can call me Tibs there beautiful." He whispers in my ears, so low I'm certain it was for my ears alone. His words cause my heart to pick up speed, and my body to quiver.

Chapter 2

<u>Annabeth</u>

A We have been here for a few hours now; I have met so many people all the faces have kind of just blurred together as one. I haven't seen Tiberius since he helped me from the car. In fact, I haven't seen too many teenagers around tonight. Every time I get glance at someone who looked to be my age, a new adult would step in front of me. Introduce themselves and talk with me for a few minutes. Then, by the time they walked away the person around my age was nowhere to be seen.

"Darling," I feel my mother's hand on the middle of my back, as she bends closer to my ear, "Could you at least fake a smile while we are here." I can hear the disappointment in her tone. Without a word, I do as she asks, smiling so big my jaw hurts. "Thank you." She whispers with a false sugary sweet tone. I nod at her and walk as far away as I can.

As I walk by people, all the strangers' faces mold into one, but I do my daughterly duty and keep the smile plastered on my lips. Until I make it around the corner, out of sight, and then I lean against the wall. Closing my eyes, I take a few deep breaths trying to get my baring. When I open my eyes, I go to plaster on another fake smile, as I take a step in the direction of the main room, when something catches my eye.

There, standing a few feet away from me, in the dark stands a boy about my age, glaring at me. I suppose I shouldn't call him a boy; he's built like a man. He has muscles that go on for days, not too built, but just enough. I can see from the lighting he's got deep brown hair, that almost looks black, gorgeous blue-green eyes, and the same beautiful plump lips as Tiberius.

If I thought he was good looking, this profound man takes the cake. I find myself growing wet between my legs just standing here looking at him. I shake my head, trying to clear my mind of those thoughts. I haven't ever thought that way before, I'm only sixteen. *So why am I feeling like this now just looking at this man?*

A carnal smirk works its way onto his gorgeous lips, before I see him step back into the dark of the unlit hallway behind him. I walk over to where he is, almost expecting him to reach out for me, grabbing me from the darkness, but to my dismay he's no longer there. I turn in a circle, looking in every direction, but I don't find him to be anywhere in the vicinity. *That's strange.*

Thinking perhaps I was only imagining things, I turn and begin walking back to the main room, where everyone is, but stop dead in my tracks. Looking out into the room full of extravagant strangers, many of them carry themselves as though they are better than everyone else, I realize how much I do not wish to be around them a moment longer. Deciding better of it, I turn around and head down the dark hallway into the unknown.

I find many rooms, that are all similar in looks. They each are spacious; I can see a king size bed in some while others have old furniture inside. Each room has high ceilings, I find I have to tilt my head back to look at them. They are beautiful, and phenomenal for sure, but I can't help feeling like it's a waste of space. By the sixth room, I find something entirely different. This room looks to be an office, the size of the room and ceilings are the same, but this one has a mahogany desk in the center, with a large chair behind it.

There are a couple couches in the room, and some chairs. Behind the desk is a wall to ceiling bookshelf. Deciding, I have nothing better to do, along with the fact I love books, I sneak into the room and quietly close the door behind me. I take a close look at all the books held in the room, and many of them are classics.

I smile at the titles, wishing I had these beauties in my possession. My shoulders fold with a wave of disappointment. It's hitting me I have to go back to the party and leave all these behind. Turning around, the phone on the desk catches my eye. I look from the closed door, back to the phone, before I decide to heck with it.

Sitting at the desk, I pick up the phone and dial the number I know by heart. I listen to it ringing, wishing for him to pick up. I really need to hear his voice. "Hello." My grandfather's raspy voice says from the other side of the line. Causing me to instantly smile, I always feel better hearing him. "Grandpa it's me."

"Annie Bannanie, my baby girl." His nickname for me makes my smile grow. I can't help but laugh. "It's me pops. I just needed to call and say hello." I call him what I have since I was five years old. I'm not sure what made me refer to him as pops, but it just felt right.

"How is the school honey. You getting along with the other kids?" I can't help my playful eyeroll at his use of "kids" as he says. To him everyone younger than him, even by a year is a kid. "I haven't really met anyone yet pops. I'm here at one of Arthur's friends' houses, and I snuck away." I nibble my bottom lip. Waiting to see if he reprimands me.

All he does is laugh loudly in my ear. All my worries and stress just melt away with the sound. What can I say? I have always been a grandpa's girl. He's been the only constant in my life that has always understood me and loved me unconditionally.

Chapter 3

E zekiel

The sound of the old man's laughter on the other line of the phone has my interest piqued. I can tell, from my spot I'm sitting at in the chair on the opposite side of her, that she is extremely close with the man. When my father told me we would be meeting a new addition to our pack, humans none the less, I couldn't help but lift my upper lip in a snarl. It's preposterous to think about.

Two human women, living amongst our kinds, I don't know what Arthur was thinking. These two have no idea the kind of world they have stepped into. My mother's kind, the werewolves, aren't the kind type. Us werewolves have a temper, some more than others. We wolf out at unexpected times, challenging one another for dominance quite often.

Don't get me started on my father's kind in our world. The witches and warlocks are nothing but conniving monsters during the day. Using our powers for a lot of manipulation, ways to get things to go how we like, and to get everything our way. Some even use it to their advantage for the small things.

I, myself, am half of each. I have the royal blood on both sides of the family. Our world, for the witches and warlocks, are made up of the four royal courts. Although, one has diminished immensely. There are Sebastian's, which is my frenemy Tiberius' family. They run things on the West Coast of America. The Barlowe's family, they control the Midwest. Unfortunately, they are the most annoying family out of everyone. Jizelle, the granddaughter to the one in charge is obsessed with me.

I roll my eyes just thinking about her. She's here somewhere tonight, I've been doing what I can to hide from her. Shaking my head, I rid thoughts of the annoyance, as I think of my family. The Whitlock's, we control the eastern shore. Which is why everyone has flown to our mansion, making themselves at home, to meet the newcomers. Speaking of which I listen in to the rest of her conversation.

"I'm good. I miss you though. How's Midnight doing?" Her eyes grow sad with the question.

"She's doing honey. I know she misses you riding her. Without you constantly getting her, she's stuck in the horse stall while I work." I see her shoulders slump from his words. I lean back in the chair, lifting one foot over my knee. I bring my hand up to my chin, relaxing with my head tilt to the side, studying her.

Her shoulders raise up as she places a fake smile on her face, "Well I better get going pops. I have more people to meet." She is trying to put on a brave face. Trick herself into thinking she will enjoy the rest of this evening meeting all these horrid beings.

"Okay, Annie Bananie. I love you with all my heart." I hear the old man's voice break on the last of his words. "I love you too pops." I can see she's trying to hold back tears, while she hangs up the phone. Once she is sitting there, alone in the dark, from her perspective anyway, she finally lets a tear drop fall. I watch as she wipes it from her cheek.

I shake my head in disgust at her human weakness. If she plans to survive in our world, she needs to develop a backbone. The people of our world are going to eat her up, chew her bones, and spit what's left of her out. There will be no way she will make it out alive once she starts at our boarding school.

I make a noise of disdain, causing her to jump in her seat. She turns in my direction, facing the man of her nightmares. A cruel smile forms along my lips. I can't help thinking of all the fun I will have with this pitiful human girl. I'm going to make her life a living hell for the next year.

"Who's there?" She jumps up from my father's chair, her hand at her chest. I can't hold back the laughter that falls from my mouth. Sitting up in the chair, I move my face into the moonlight that is in the room from the window. I fold my hands between my spread legs, looking up at her through the few strands of my hair that have fallen forward.

"Didn't mean to startle you little lamb." The nickname drips from my lips. I didn't mean to call her anything like that, but the words feel right for her. She is now a lamb in a world full of wolves. She looks around the darkened room, looking for the door to escape the room if need be. She places a piece of her auburn hair behind her ear, swallowing her fear.

"And you are?" She raises her chin in a challenging way. Causing my wolf to pace back and forth within my head. This may be a lot more fun than I anticipated.

Her head tilts to the side, I find her studying me just as closely as I am her. "I'm Ezekiel Whitlock." I sit back in the chair once more, lifting my leg over my knee. I hold out my hands "You can call me Master." The words fall from my lips, the seduction of my tone apparent. I don't know what it is with this human girl, but I find I have to bite my bottom lip to keep quiet around her, or I may just talk dirty to her all night. A carnal smile forms on my lips at the thought.

Chapter 4

A nnabeth
    I don't know who this guy thinks he is. *"You can call me master." Is he insane?* My thoughts must show on my face because as I'm stuck in my own head he laughs out loud. The noise doing weird things to my body. I would like to say the sound is making my skin crawl, but it's doing the complete opposite. Goose bumps are on my skin going up my entire arm. My legs feel like Jell-O, and I'm fighting the need to lean my head back and moan out loud.

What the hell is wrong with me? Get it together Annabeth! I chastise myself, as I straighten my shoulders and look at him head on.

"A little tip," I tilt my head to the side. His eyes meet mine from across the room. If I didn't have his attention before, my snarky tone gained it now. "Don't hold your breath waiting for me to call you that. You may very well die." I make sure to make my tone sound sugary sweet.

Judging by the solemn look that built on his face, he didn't like my words at all. He brings his hand to his chin, as he studies me even closer, he rubs his thumb across that delectable bottom lip of his. I'm not certain what he's thinking about, but I wish I could read minds right now. I hear him hum, before he drops his hand to the arm of the chair. In one swift motion, he stands at his full height, and takes a step in my direction.

Before I can get my bearings, he's standing in front of me, so close our noses are almost touching. I want to tell him to back up, but I'm stuck trying to wrap my head around how he made it to me so quickly. "Little lamb, mark my words," he steps even closer to me. Causing me to take a step back, only I don't get very far. The mahogany desk is at my back. He takes advantage, bringing his arms up, on each side of me, caging me in.

His body leans into mine, and it makes me crazy that I can feel the steady beat of his heart against me. It's as though he's completely calm at the moment, whereas I am a mess. My palms have grown sweaty, my heart is accelerating, and I'm shaking immensely. All from a simple close proximity to the man standing in front of me. He keeps me on the precipice as he sniffs the side of my face, so close to my neck, I find myself biting down on my bottom lip, trying not to make a noise. If I do that perhaps he won't know how he weirdly affects me.

He holds his face there for a moment, just breathing me in. "You need to back up." I'm trying for a strong approach, hoping my tone conveys how serious I am. Hopefully, it'll stop whatever is happening between us right now. Clearly, it doesn't work. He's still standing in front of me, caging me between the desk and his body, sniffing my neck. When I feel the wetness of his tongue along my skin, that gets me into action.

"Too far," I push his upper body away from me. To my shock, he allows it. I can feel the muscles of his body below my hand, telling me just how built he is. If he didn't want to move, there would be no way I would have been able to force him to.

"I don't even know you. This scare tactic of yours is unnecessary, but you are licking my skin as though I am your property in which you feel you have the right to do anything to me is overboard." He looks down at where my hand is laying upon his chest.

My eyes follow his line of vision, slowly I move my hand away from his body. I hadn't noticed I had kept it there after pushing him away. Before I can bring my hand close to my own body, and hold it away from his view, he latches onto it. Holding it in the air, held tight with his own. His eyes move from our join hands to my face, starting at my lips, and I watch them slowly make their way to my eyes.

When he is looking right into my blue eyes, I have to close my mouth before I find myself begging him to touch me. My feelings are all over the place. I feel like a conundrum, feeling injustice in one moment, and a wanton slut the next. A devious smile forms on his lips, as he brings our hands to his mouth. He kisses each of my fingertips one by one, not breaking eye contact with me the entire time.

"Haven't you learned anything from tonight little lamb?" He asks as he bites the tip of my pointer finger.

The nickname he has given me, I am despising more and more by the second. I want to tell him so, but every time I open my mouth no words come out. Just little noises, that I hadn't known I could make. Causing him to smile, a genuine one at that, all his straight white teeth showing in the dark.

He places my hand down onto the top of the desk, and crowds into my body once more. I find I cannot look at him, I'm too afraid of what I might do. I look down at his chest, realizing that even through the button-down shirt he's wearing I can make out every crevice of his muscular chest. I find I want to touch him more than I want oxygen right now.

"No, no little lamb." His hand shoots out and grabs my chin. He forces my eyes up to his blue green ones. The look on his face has turned carnal, like a wolf hunting its prey. I know from that look held in his eyes, if I were to look away again, he would strike. How? I'm not certain, but the feeling of dread coursing through my veins, has me not moving an inch.

"When we converse, you will look me in the eye. Always!" The last word comes out deadly quiet. I swear I heard a hint of a growl by the end of his sentence. I don't comment on that, no I just stand there, like a deer caught in headlights. Giving this crazy man my full attention.

"You may not like it, but in our world, you are at the bottom of the food chain. Meaning when I tell you to call me something," He brings his face so close our lips are a hair breadth away from one another. "You will call me said name." He tilts my chin upward, making it so our lips are barely touching one another. If someone were to walk in, they may think we were kissing, but we aren't. At least I don't think we are.

I haven't ever been kissed in my life, hell this is the most interaction I've had with the opposite sex. "If I tell you to do something, no matter how degrading, you will do it. That's the way of the world you now live in." With every word that falls from his mouth, his lips move across my own. I'm tempted to open my mouth and tell this man off, but a bigger part of me wants to reach around and pull him closer. So, I can really taste him.

Once his words really hit me, I find his words to be confusing. *What does he mean in the world I now live in? With the rich and powerful?* Just as I'm about to open my mouth and ask him, I hear the door open, and the room is filled with light. I try to push him away, not wanting anyone to see us in this predicament, but this time Ezekiel doesn't allow it.

Chapter 5

Ezekiel

The weak human tries her hardest to pull away from me, but for some strange reason I'm not ready for there to be a slither of distance between us. It pisses me off! Once the door is completely open, I think about humiliating her. By shoving her away, so she falls back into the chair, and turning to walk away. My plans change when I get a whiff of who our company is. Instead, I pull her that much closer to me and take her mouth with mine.

I hear an aggravated growl come from Tiberius, as I hear a feminine voice scoff at my actions. At first the little human is frozen stiff, her hands laid beside her, which I have to admit to myself I don't very much care for. Once I lick her lips with the tip of my tongue, to my utter enjoyment she opens for my onslaught. I attack her mouth giving her everything I have. All the pent-up aggression and heat from the last couple of hours gets poured into this kiss.

She begins delving her tongue into my mouth right back, wrestling for dominance. When her arms wrap around my neck, I can't help the excited growl working it's way up my throat as a fire burns through my body. Before long, my hands find their way to her ass. I grab a handful of those sweet cheeks of hers, that I've been watching all night, and pick her body up, slamming her down on top of my father's desk. She spreads her legs wide, making more than enough room for me to work my way in.

I hadn't planned to do anything remotely like this with the girl. My plan was to be as cruel as I could be to her tonight. Causing her to cry and leave the room. So, she would be begging her mother to let her go and live with her grandfather, back where she belongs, and far away from my kind. To remove her from my world, so the temptation would go away along with her. Instead, I find me rubbing my very hard cock against her pelvic area, making her moan, and the sounds she is making driving me insane.

I find my wolf wants nothing more than to rip her clothes completely from her body and slide into her delectably sweet pussy.

"I think that's enough." The sound of Jizelle's voice makes my once hardened cock lose some of its momentum. Don't get me wrong the girl is drop dead gorgeous, but the moment she opens her mouth and words come out it makes me go soft in a second.

The little human must have heard her, remembering we are not alone, as she brings her hands to my shoulders and tries to push me away from her once more. I find it's more difficult to move away from her than I'd like to admit. I don't know what it is about this human, but she makes me crave things that are impossible to have.

Once our lips are no longer connected, I find it easier to shove her away from me. She falls backwards along my father's desk, looking up at me with both confusion and ture fear held within her eyes. Good! She needs to be afraid of me and hate me so she will stay far away. Without breaking eye contact with her, a sly smile forms on my lips as I make it known to the entire room, "Couldn't help myself. Needed a little taste of the newbie." My tone is predatory.

I make a show of looking at her body as though she's my next meal. If our audience were to leave the room, she very well may be. I Start from the tips of her toes that are in those sexy high heels her mother forced her to wear, all the way up her long legs, that are smooth as butter, to her hips and flat stomach. I pause a moment on her chest area, this girl has the most gorgeous Double D's I have ever seen. Licking my lips, I bite my bottom lip thinking of all the things I will be doing to them. Once I have my fill, I make my way up to her throat. The area I must stay away from at all costs, no questions asked about that.

Finally, I make my way up to her face, I study those pillowy lips of hers. The ones I know I will be biting a lot to get a little taste of her from time to time. Her cute button nose, that have a row of freckles scattered all along it and her cheeks. Finally, I make my way up to her beautiful sky-blue eyes. They are still dilated from our little display we just shared. I can see her chest rising and falling with every breath she takes.

When her arousal hits my nose, I know my wolf came to the forefront, as her eyes grow large. She sits up from her position on the desk and goes to stand to be closer to me once more. I move away from her, leaving her standing there with her hand held out. I know she wanted to touch my face, to see if my eyes had really turned gold and glowed in the dark room. She shakes her head, trying to work out what she just saw. Knowing I need to put a stop to this, I lean against the bookshelf behind the desk.

Rubbing my bottom lip with my thumb, I shrug my shoulders, "She wasn't too bad, but I doubt I'll ever want to kiss her again. She lacks the experience I like in a woman." I raise up to my full height and bring my face close to her ear. "You're just a little girl trying to be a woman, aren't you?" I whisper to her. I hear her intake of breath at my words.

When I pulled back, she surprises me. Her hand raises and makes contact with my cheek. I find she doesn't have a bad swing as my head moves slightly to the side. I take a moment to calm down, before bringing my eyes back to her once more. I glare down at her, but all she does is glare right back. "You're a special kind of asshole." She whisper yells at me, before shoving me away from her. This time I allow it, as I watch as she stomps her feet so hard, I'm almost afraid she may break her heals.

She walks around to the front of the desk, shoves Tiberius and Jizelle out of her way, and makes her way down the hall. I can feel their eyes on me, but I pay them no mind. My full attention is on my little lamb that just left the room.

"You're such a dick." Tiberius scoffs, shaking his head at me. He turns and walks out the door, to follow the little human I assume.

That thought makes my blood boil with rage. I can feel my fingers curl into fists as I try to keep myself in the same spot. So, I don't chase after the both of them and rip Tiberius to shreds.

Jizelle simply gives me that evil smirk of hers. The one everyone knows, before she winks at me and walks out the door. I can hear her laughter echo down the hall. I simply walk to my father's mini bar he has in the room. Pour myself a shot of bourbon, enjoying the burn as the liquid makes its way down my throat. I stand here looking out at the night sky for all of five minutes before I say fuck it and decide to chase.

Chapter 6

Annabeth
    I ran as fast as I could, trying to get away from that office. Where *he* is. I have no idea what I had done wrong. He really seemed to enjoy that kiss just as much as I had. It wasn't just a chaste kiss, peck on the lips, or anything remotely close to that. It was pure passion. His hands were all over my body. Starting in my hair, down my back, and he even grabbed my ass. I mean cupped both cheeks in his hands, and lifted me clear in the air, slamming me on that desk.

Am I just supposed to believe that he felt nothing? Although I clearly did when I spread my legs for him like a hussy, and he took the invitation I handed him with glee. He was rock hard against my lady bits, and it felt amazing. Hell, I am still wet between my legs with all the rubbing we had done.

Realizing I am almost back in the ballroom, where all the boring people are, and my mother I come to a screeching halt. Looking around the room in the dark, I can see her standing by the punch bowl with Arthur. He seems to be chastising her, I can tell even from this distance that she isn't happy. She's trying to play it off as nothing, she has on that fake smile, the one she's had plastered on her face since the day she met him.

"Oh man, the aggression coming off of you in waves is unbearable." I see out of the corner of my eye, someone waving their hand in the air. The voice causes me to turn my head to get a better look at who it is. Tiberius stands there, with a twinkle in his eye as he looks at me. He brings his hands into his slack pockets, as his chin goes down to touch his shirt. "You want to go for a walk in the garden?" His question throws me off, I'm not so used to anyone of the opposite sex talking with me, let alone kissing me.

Shaking my head, I try to forget about that disaster for a moment, smile at him and give a small nod. He smiles so bright; I can see all his teeth. He turns his body more, folding his arm out to me. "My lady," with his other he holds palm out in a dramatic way. Causing a small laugh to leave my body, as I curl my arm into his. "Thank you, kind sir."

"Please, I work for a living." He laughs at his own joke, as we walk farther down the hallway, taking turn after turn, and making us grow a safe distance from everyone at the party. When we make it to some double doors, he releases my arm, and with a wink my way, he opens both doors at once. Causing my breath to hitch at what I see. I would almost think it was a winter wonderland.

The garden is beautiful! It's filled with the most gorgeous flowers I have ever seen. Wrapped around each tree that stands in the center, are different color lights. Some blue, green, red, and gold are blinking away.

"Shall we?" He walks to my side once more and takes my hand with his. It came out as a question, but the way he's tugging me close behind him, he's not giving me a lot of a choice.

Ezekiel

I have to take a deep breath, as I watch the two of them make their way into the garden. I feel so beyond pissed, that I can feel my claws are out, scratching the hell out of the palm of my hand. It doesn't matter, hell I don't even feel it. All I feel, is annoyance, and something I haven't ever felt before. I don't even know how to describe it.

All I know for certain is I want to follow them out there, ripping Tiberius to shreds, and lift the girl over my shoulder. Claiming my prize, running off with the human, and getting as far away from here as we can. I don't know what is happening to me, but I'm not enjoying this at all.

"You can do so much better. I mean, she's not even that pretty if you ask me." Jizelle says somewhere behind me.

"No one asked you. Nor do I give a shit what you think." I hear her snide little laugh, as I feel the heat of her body hit my back. Letting me know she's too close for comfort.

"I can make you forget all about the weak, ugly human. That is now a part of our pack thanks to my stupid uncle." She spits her poison out so calmly, as I feel her hand makes its way up my arm.

"Come on. Give me one chance to show you what I can do. I know you'll love it." That's it! I've heard enough. I brush her arm off of me and turn my head to the side. So, she can see the redness of my eyes.

My angry growl has a good effect on her. She falls to her knees, bowing her head she begs for my forgiveness. "Go suck Johnny off or Luca. They both love your company." I wave her off, but to my annoyance she doesn't move.

"I don't want them. You are the only one I crave." She looks up at me through her black hair, "It has always been you. Why do you think I do what I do with the others?"

With a shrug of my shoulders, I turn away from her, giving all my focus to Annabeth. She is spinning around in front of the fountain, holding her hands in the air, laughing. That noise makes my ears twitch. I see Tiberius sitting his ass on the fountain, looking at her, well studying her is more like it. Just as I am doing. I can see by the way he is looking at her, he's interested.

"Ezekiel, please listen to me. I want to please you, and I know how now." Jizelle has her hand along my arm, tugging it to get my attention.

"You have five seconds to get away from me before I really lose my patience." With my low tone, she knows I mean it. I hear her sniff, can smell the saltiness of her tears, as she turns and runs down the hallway.

With her gone I bring all my attention to my little lamb. She looks happy, too happy for my liking. When Tiberius stands up and places his hand along her hip that's my cue to make myself known. He shouldn't be touching her. She's mine to touch, mine to torment. I am the only one that can make her feel anything and know the feel of her skin below my hand. No one else will have that pleasure!

Chapter 7

A <u>nnabeth</u>
   I'm twirling around like a young girl again. I can't help myself; this garden is one of the most beautiful places I have ever seen. All the beautiful colors of the flowers, the lights twinkling in the dark, with the moon light shining down on me. I close my eyes and breathe in the night.

My eyes pop open when I feel heat from a hand along my hip. Turning my head to the side, I can see Tiberius standing beside me, his blue eyes twinkling with mischief. I want to be comfortable with him, really, I do, but I find I don't like his touch as much as Ezekiel's. There must be something wrong with me.

I give him my best fake smile, the one I have perfected over the last few months. When his own falls slowly from his face, I know he can see right through my demeanor.

"I'm sorry," I close my mouth a second later, not sure what I'm apologizing for, only that I feel the need to. He shrugs his shoulders once more, a bright smile on his face.

"Don't worry about it. No need to apologize." I can tell by the look in his eyes, he means what he says.

The next second, I can see his demeanor change entirely. His shoulders fall, "Ezekiel. What do we owe for the pleasure of your presence?" He removes his hand from my hip. I had entirely forgotten it was there. I take a deep breath, before turning around to face the boy that makes my heart beat faster, my palms get sweaty, and my knees grow weak.

I find myself stepping back, as far away from him as I can get, because the look on his face says it all. He's beyond pissed off, and he's determined to bring someone pain. I just hope it's not me, I've already been hurt by him enough the few hours I have known him. Tiberius steps in front of me, blocking his view of me entirely.

21

I don't know what is going on over his shoulder, but I can tell from the aggravated growl that comes from both men it's not good.

"Move now Tib, or you will not like what I do next." I hear Ezekiel whisper low. What has me confused is it doesn't sound like him at all. Sounds more like a beast speaking out loud.

I watch as he steps away, holding out his hand towards where I stand. I turn to flee, but there's nothing but a fence in wall behind me.

"Shit, I went the wrong way." I curse the heavens above for my insolence. When I feel a hand land on my shoulder, I turn around ready to punch him if he dares try to do something to me.

As I turn around, everything happens so quickly, before I know what's happening, he has my arms held at my sides, with his body so close to mine, we are practically breathing together. To my surprise he doesn't look angry if anything he has a sad look in his eyes.

"Don't ever hit me. I don't want you to get hurt." Before I can ask him what he means, he takes my hand with his, and pulls me along behind him.

I find myself, following close behind his back, not saying a word. I can see Tiberius standing to the side, his arms crossed over his chest, and an angry look in his eyes.

"You can't just claim her you know! She's not yours!" He hollers after us. I turn to look at him one last time, but Ezekiel speeding up has my attention facing forward. Trying to make sure I don't bump into anything, or worse fall flat on my face. Embarrassing myself in front of the infuriating man dragging me behind him.

Ezekiel

I walk faster as I hear Tiberius yell at me. I know she looked back at him, and I don't like it one bit. I go a little faster, to make sure she faces me once more. I know he isn't wrong; this girl is not mine, but I can't find myself to stop the craziness that has taken over my body tonight.

I pull her along, through the hallways of the house, to the front doors. The guards there open them up, nodding their heads at me. One has an eyebrow raised, I know he is wondering what I'm doing with the poor, confused woman I'm dragging behind me. I also know they are smart enough not to question me.

I walk her down the long and winding stairs at the side, leading her to the houses along the side of the house. They will be staying at the first one to our right, I made sure of that. I need her close to me, when I saw her picture for some reason something about her called to me like a siren. I needed to know she was in my arms reach.

"Ezekiel, where are you taking me." It's the first time I have heard her speak for the last few minutes. I don't answer her though, I simply turn to the house, walking her up the two steps onto the porch. Once we are at the door, I pull out the key wrapped around my neck, opening it up. I pull her in the house behind me. I pushed her further into the room. Without turning around, I kick the door closed behind us.

I stand here for a moment, breathing harder with each second that passes. Trying to calm my wolf, he wants to come to the forefront right now. It's not a good idea, there is no telling what I'll do to the fragile woman that stands before me. I can scent both confusion and fear in the air surrounding her.

That's what has me needing to calm down before I lift my head to look at her. I never want her to fear me in this way, so I need to take a few breaths, calm my ass down before I say what needs to be said. She needs to know my rules, the ones for the world she now lives in.

"You're scaring me." I hear her say softly.

I can hear her stepping closer and closer to where I stand. I have my head bent down, both my hands at my side turning into fists, my legs spread wide. I lay my head back with my eyes closed, counting the steps, listening intently for when she will be right in front of me.

I fight with myself right now; I know I need her touch more than anything. She is the only one that can calm all the raging thoughts working their way through my mind, but there is another part of me that dreads when she does. That part of me wants to do very bad things right now, and I'm not so certain I'll be able to hold myself back.

Chapter 8

A<u>nnabeth</u>
I don't fully understand what is going on here and looking around I have no idea where we are. He pulled me along, right into this house, that has furniture already in it. What I can see with the little moonlight through the window, it has nothing but white walls. He's facing me head on, his arms stretched at his sides. His shoulders are moving up and down with every breath he takes.

I'm sure this is stupid of me, but after I whisper out loud that he's scaring me, I feel my feet moving towards him. Closing my eyes, I pray to the God's I'm not as stupid as I feel right now. Opening them I reach my hand to touch his face. My fingers are just an inch away from touching him, and I brace myself.

I don't know what it is with him, but whenever we make contact, I feel a spark work its way through my entire body. I don't know what it is, but it scares the hell out of me.

"Ezekiel, can you please talk to me and explain." I say just as I touch his cheek.

I have this immense feeling, but I don't have a lot of time to process it. One second, I'm standing before him, my hand on his face, and the next he grabs ahold of me. Turning our bodies around and slamming my back against the door.

His hands latch onto mine, our fingers entwined together, as he stretches both our arms above our heads.

"Zeek." He mutters. My brows furrow with that one word.

"Call me Zeek, I hate my full name." He explains with a devilish smile on his lips. Closing my mouth, I swallow down the questions I want to ask more than anything right now. The way he's looking at me has a puddle forming at my center.

His eyes begin staring into mine, he's looking at my face like I'm a mystery he wishes desperately he can figure out. His eyes make their way to my neck, I see him focus on my heartbeat there.

His tongue makes its way out of his mouth as he licks his lips. The next moment, he's bringing his face close to my body. I can hear him breathing heavily. That's when I realize he's breathing in my scent.

"Fuck, you are my new addiction." I hear him whisper lightly along my skin.

I turn my head to the side making it easier for him. I feel his tongue along my skin, as he licks the entirety of my skin there. From my collar bone all the way up to behind my ear. Once there, he lightly bites the tip of my ear, causing a moan to work its way up my throat.

"Do you know how much I hate you right now?" His question is contradictive to his actions.

He's the one that cannot keep his hands off me. Not that I'm complaining in the least. I find when it comes to him, I become a little hussy, secretly hoping he'll never stop touching me. He pulls away from me, glaring down at me.

The girl from the office wants to look down or to the side. Anywhere as long as it's not at him, but instead I find myself straightening my shoulders. Raising my chin, a little higher, looking him dead on.

"Your body says otherwise." I whisper at him as I roll my hips along his hardened cock.

For a brief second, he closes his eyes, when they open back up, I could have sworn they turned a yellow color and glowed in the dark. I try to reach my hand out to touch his face, but he tightens his hold on my wrists. Closing his eyes once more, he shakes his head from side to side, and when he opens them back up again his eyes are back to the blue green shade that I have fallen in love with tonight.

Ezekiel

She's playing with fire, pushing all the wrong buttons, and she don't even know it. She keeps this up, I may not be able to hold myself back. I have to! I cannot let her make me weak in any way. If I give into my basic instincts, I'll plow deep into her delicious body, there will be no escape for her. She's not ready for that, hell I'm not prepared for it myself in the least. I like having all the women I want, the money, the power. I don't need this human coming in here and fucking everything up.

I drop her arms, hearing them fall at her sides, as I shove away from her. Turning around I give her my back.

"This is the house your mother and Arthur will be living in." I walk to the opposite wall, lean my back against it, as I take my cigarettes and lighter from my pocket. I light one up, taking a puff deep into my lungs, I blow the smoke out from my nose. Studying her, as she takes in the room.

"You shouldn't do that. It's bad for your health." Her nose bunches up as she points to the offensive tobacco filled goodness I hold in my hand.

"Don't worry about it. I'll be fine." I tell her truthfully. I can't get a normal human disease like cancer or anything like that. We witch, warlocks, and werewolves are immune to every disease known to man.

"It's your body, your choice." She shrugs her shoulders at me looking away once more.

"This is where I'll be staying and commuting to my new school?" I can't help myself; I laugh at her question. One that holds absolutely no humor.

"No little lamb, this is just where you stay for tonight. Tomorrow we all go to our boarding school that is two hours away." I lift my foot to put out the cigarette.

I place the butt of the cigarette in my pocket, as I walk towards her. She takes a step to the side, trying to get out of my way. I pause for a moment and study her out of the corner of my eye.

"You afraid of me Lamb?" I turn my body towards her and take another step in her direction. She takes one back, refusing to look at me.

We continue this little dance of ours until the back of her legs hit the couch, causing her to fall on her ass. Once she's seated on the cushion, I make my way to her body, kneeling directly in front of her.

She places her hands on my shoulders, trying and failing miserably to shove me away from her. I simply sit there, allowing her to continue until finally she gets the hint. I will move when I wish to.

"You don't have to be. I wouldn't actually hurt you," I reach my hand out and grab her chin.

Bringing her face close to mine I whisper along her lips, "Not physically anyway."

Chapter 9

Annabeth

He takes my hands with his, as he stares down at them, I have to focus on my breathing. I don't know what he's doing to me right now, but my body feels alive. Almost like I have been electrocuted. My breathing is picking up as his fingers rub along mine, goosebumps have formed on my legs and arms. In this position, with him kneeling in front of me, he's so close to the spot on my body that cries out for him, it's making me want to squirm.

I don't though, afraid any sudden movement will make him run away. Within seconds, he is moving his body up closer to mine, his hands slam down to the side of my body. He places my hands on the cushions, looking deep into my eyes.

"Keep them there." He says as he looks deep into my eyes. I have to swallow down my panic, not knowing what he has planned.

When he moves his hands away from mine, I don't move causing a devious smile to form along his lips. This young man kneeling in front of me is as deadly as a shark when he looks at someone, but with that smile on his lips it makes him look like an Angel. I have to remember who he is, not letting that look cloud my judgement. I have to keep my walls up.

"Good girl." He whispers close to my lips.

I'm not meaning to be submissive right now, it just naturally happens when he's around me. I can't explain it. I'm taken from my thoughts when he begins moving his face slowly down my body. I'm feeling so worked up, my breasts almost touch his lips with every breath I take as he runs along my body.

He looks up at me through the little bit of hair that has fallen in front of his eyes. I can see a smirk on his lips, as he moves an inch closer and kisses my left breast above my shirt. A light moan works its way up my throat, he must like the sound as an animalistic noise comes from his own.

"Keep those eyes open and on me lamb." His words have me so worked up, I want to move my hips to gain friction.

I hadn't even realized my eyes had closed. They must have with the sensations that are coursing through my body. They pop open, and he's no longer down near my breasts, but back up right in my face. I want to move my body back, getting some space between us, but I find I can't move in the slightest.

"Keep them open and on me, or I'll stop what I'm doing. Leaving you wanting and needy for the rest of the night." His words cause my heartbeat to plummet.

Nodding my head, I let him know I will try my best to look at him from now on. He looks between my eyes, and must like what he sees there, as he pecks me on the lips, and begins going down my body once more.

As he makes it to my breasts, he looks up at me. I'm expecting him to give my right one a fleeing kiss, but he surprises me by covering the entirety of into his mouth. My legs open wide, giving him better access to move his body between there and come even closer.

With one hand he plays with the other breast, as he devours the other over my shirt. It's not skin on skin contact, but it feels amazing just the same. I want to grind against him, but he's keeping the lower part of him further away from me. I believe he's doing it on purpose if the twinkle in his eye tells me anything about it.

Ezekiel

She's driving me crazy, I'm doing everything I can to keep our clothes on right now, but all I am dying to do is tear them away and sink deep inside of her. I know she craves the friction, of my lower region against hers. I'm purposely keeping a small distance between us down there. I need to make her want me as much as I do her.

I hate myself for being this weak around one young woman. Normally, I don't give a flying fuck about any of them that come and go. They are just to help me get a release, then we get dressed, and go our separate ways. Seldom, do I take one girl more than once. I don't need any of them getting the wrong idea. I'm not boyfriend material. I wouldn't know the first things about that.

The only role models I've ever had are my parents, and they married for the power. Not for love. In fact, my father sat me down at the young age of ten, explaining to me how love can make you weak. That he forbids me to ever have true feelings for a female. No son of his will be weak in this world.

I took his word at heart, by making sure I don't get close to anyone. I have responsibilities in my family, meaning I cannot show a hint of weakness. So, once I hit thirteen, I began sleeping with any woman I found pretty enough. Hell, I don't even look them in the face, taking them from behind so there are no emotions at all.

This is the closest I have ever been to a woman, and it's exciting my wolf, and terrifying me. Getting out of my thoughts, I look at the top of her shirt, seeing six buttons at the top, I raise one hand and begin undoing them. When she doesn't stop me after the first comes undone, I continue on with the rest.

This opens her shirt just above her breasts, giving me perfect access for what I have planned. I release her breast from my mouth, looking deep into her eyes, I begin moving towards the skin showing just above my head. I look at her the entire time, looking for any discomfort or for her to tell me no.

When she doesn't, I lick her skin, dipping my tongue into the crevice of her open shirt. She's breathing heavy now, I know she's as wet as the ocean right now. I can smell her need in the air. It's making my wolf pace back and forth in my head. I move her shirt a little to the side, kissing the tops of each breast, before I force myself to move further down her body.

If I stay focused up there, I'm bound to do something she's not ready for tonight. I kiss along her stomach above her shirt, from left to right once I reach her hips, and stop once I'm just above her sweet spot.

"You want me to continue?" My voice comes out breathy. I am feeling things I've never felt before and I don't like it.

She nods her head, and I watch as her little tongue licks her lips to wet them. "Close your eyes." As she does, I kiss just above where she needs me the most, knowing full well what she'll do. Sure enough, her hands move to the back of my head, her fingers running through my hair. The next second, I stand to my full height, giving her my back, I walk to the door.

"What the fuck." I hear her whisper yell at me from behind. When I reach for the door, I turn the knob, opening it slightly. I turn to face her, giving her my most devious smile.

"I told you not to move your hands. You disobeyed." I say with a shrug of my shoulders. I shoot her a wink as I make my way onto the porch.

"You asshole!" I see her stand from the couch out of the corner of my eye. I slam the door just as she makes it there and run down the steps into the grass. I hear the door open, and her curse me to hell. I do nothing but laugh the whole way to my room.

Chapter 10

<u>Annabeth</u>
A   I sit in the passenger seat of my mother's car, staring out the window. I watch the trees pass us by with every mile we get further and further away from the Whitlock's mansion. Well should I call it that or is it more of a sanctuary?

I mean it's a humongous house, but there's like a little village on their land where everyone lives. My brows must be furrowed, as I'm trying to think this all out in my head because my mother says from beside me, "You shouldn't allow your face to strain darling. It's not good for the complexion."

I have to stop myself from rolling my eyes at the woman that sits beside me. It's a battle I find I have continuously lost these last few months. Looking at her out of the corner of my eye, I study the stranger beside me. She's nothing like the woman I grew up with. It's as though when Arthur came into our lives, my mother suddenly disappeared as I knew her. Replaced by this glamorous robot that spits out poison every time her mouth opens.

"Sorry, I hadn't realized I was straining my face." My voice comes out neutral, thank goodness. I don't think I can deal with one of her many lectures this early in the morning. There's silence in the vehicle for a moment, falsely leading me to believe I can lean my head back and close my eyes. Taking a breather from everything that has happened in less than twenty-four hours.

"I heard that Ezekiel and Tiberius both left quite the impression on you last night." My head lifts and eyes pop open automatically as I stare at her. Thinking the worst of what she knows. I'm certain there's about to be a talk of how I shouldn't be so promiscuous when it comes to teenage boys.

Shockingly, she releases the steering wheel to clap her hands with a gleeful laugh. Causing me to raise an eyebrow in disbelief. When she places her hands back on the wheel she begins to speak.

"This is marvelous. My darling daughter getting on both boys' radar. Oh, the possibilities are endless." My mouth falls open at the meaning of her words.

"Are you serious right now?" I ask her incredulously.

I cannot believe how little tact she has right now. Her lips purse in agitation.

"Don't you take that tone with me young lady." The sound of her turn signal echoes in my ears.

I want to say something else, but the winding paved road, leading deep into the woods has caught my attention. It takes all of ten minutes until we make it to the gate of the school.

"They must really want to keep this place hidden." I whisper to myself.

I watch as my mother rolls down her window, handing over a pile of papers I hadn't noticed before. I blame my high emotions from last night with that one. She says something quietly to the guard before he hands her the papers, and the gates are open.

"Welcome to the start of your new life darling." She's smiling so brightly at me, the shine from her straight white teeth is blinding.

Once we drive further into the establishment, I can see statues along the way. Some of fierce men surrounded by what looks to be wolves. On the opposite side, It looks like some women with their hands held up to their chests as though in prayer, or out towards the Heavens. The entire visual is odd to say the least.

When we make it to the front of the school I'm shocked at what I see. The building is made of a gray stone, and twice the size of the Whitlock mansion. There are gargoyle statues, along with more wolves around the building. I can see many people my age outside. Some are lounging around the grass and stairs, talking away without a care in the world. While others seem to be focused on papers they have right in their faces. I'm guessing they are new here too. They look just as confused as I know I will here in a moment.

"Okay," mom throws her car in park, walks around the vehicle and opens the back passenger door. Just as I unbuckle and step out she turns to face me with a shoulder bag in one hand, and my duffle bag in the other. She holds them out to me.

As I take them, she bends down to the backseat once more. I take a moment to stand there, the duffle bag by my feet, the other on my shoulder, as I study my surroundings.

"Here is your schedule, as well as your room assignment." She hands me two pieces of paper as she says this.

Closing the door, she smiles at me before giving her full attention to the building that stands before us.

"I am so jealous of you right now. If only I had this at your age." Her eyes grow sad, before she places her hand along my shoulder, and pats me there. Treating me as though I'm a stranger on the street and not her daughter.

"You're not coming with me. Just to see my room, and meet my roommate and everything?" My mother gets on my nerves big time lately, with her new holy and better than you attitude, but this is a new place for me. I stupidly expected her to be back towards my old mother just for a half hour at least, and walk me in.

Shaking her head, she looks at the teenagers surrounding us.

"No darling, Arthur is expecting me. He feels you don't need to be coddled and I agree." She gives me a slight smile, before she drops her hand away from me, and walks back to the driver's side without a backwards look at me.

"Have fun." I hear her briefly say, as she buckles in, starts the car and drives away. Just like that I'm officially on my own. Feeling like my mother doesn't even care anymore.

Chapter 11

E zekiel

I watch from my place below the trees, as that laughable woman she calls her mother leaves her to the wolves. The stupid bitch has no idea the kind of danger her little girl is truly in being here. "So, that's the human that has you and Tibs in a tizzy?" I blow the smoke from my lungs, flinging the offensive cigarette away, as I look at my best friend with an eyebrow raised.

Roman looks my way, mirroring my stance, he raises his own eyebrow and dares me to argue. We stand like that, me leaning against the tree, my leg propped up and arms folded over my chest. He is standing there with his legs spread wide, and his own monstrous arms folded.

"You telling me that I'm wrong? That girl doesn't hold your attention?" he tilts his head to the side studying me.

I don't know what to say, for some reason unbeknownst to me that weak human does in fact hold my attention. It pisses me off! He must see the look in my eyes, my answer clear on my face as he begins to boisterously laugh. "I thought so." He turns to face where she stands looking at the papers her mother handed her. "Not that I blame you. She is pretty hot."

Before I even know what I'm doing my feet are moving toward him. A growl working its way up my throat as a warning. When I step up close to him, it doesn't phase him in the least. He's the only wolf in this world not afraid of me. I'm not sure how long we stand like this, me glaring, and him fighting a crude smile.

"Hey, hey what did we miss here?" I hear footsteps coming through the path, as Leo and Deluca step into our view.

"Staring contest? I have winner." I roll my eyes and walk away from my best friend.

"Not a staring contest you dumbass." I say as I walk by him.

I see him shrug his shoulders with a laugh, "Only because you know I'd kick your ass at that game. I mean I am the greatest." He holds out his hands dramatically, nodding his tilted head.

"Still full of yourself I see." I hear his voice, making me grind my teeth together. After what he pulled last night, he has a lot of nerve showing up here right now.

"Tiberius, how was the rest of your night?" I know it's a dick move, but I can't help myself.

He was trying to put all his slimy moves on the human last night. I didn't like it one bit. He gives me a devious smile, one that holds no humor. "I went and found Jezzie to keep me company." Rolling my eyes, I can't say I'm surprised by that.

He's a worse man whore than myself. When he can't get the girl he wants for the night, he spends his night inside Jezzie. They use one another for the release. Neither really has feelings for each other. Jezzie uses him to try and get to me, thinking I'll want her if she's sleeping with my frenemy. Tiberius only uses her for a warm hole to get his dick wet. His words not mine.

"Of course, you did." I hear Deluca say in disdain.

He's the most mature of us all. Keeps the rest of us on the straight and narrow. He's one of those rare werewolves that is looking for his mate, even though that hasn't happened in well over two hundred years. I lean once more against the tree, watching this play out.

"What? I wanted someone else for a few hours, but someone ruined that last night." He glares at me.

I do nothing but wink at him, causing a growl to come from his mouth. "She's human." The sound of Deluca telling him the facts has him giving his full attention to my friend once more.

"I would have been gentle with her."

"Not the fucking point." The words fall from my mouth before Deluca can answer him.

"She knows nothing about our world and judging by how she reacted last night I would say she's clearly a virgin." My words cause his eyes to light up, as he licks his lips. I know that look, he wants her even more now.

"You are to stay as far away from her Tibs as I say. I mean it."

He takes a few steps in my direction, "Or what Zeek? You going to make me?" I laugh at his antics; I know he's trying to get a rise out of me. He always does, but nothing ever works.

"If he doesn't I sure as hell will." Deluca says out loud.

Tiberius pays him no mind, he's still staring at me, anger held deep in his eyes.

"Hey who wants to hear a joke?" Leo asks trying to cut through the tension filling the air around us.

"Sure, why not." I see Roman shrug his shoulders as he walks closer to me and Tibs.

I know he will get between the two of us if anything goes down. I hear Leo say something, but since I'm not fully listening, I don't hear everything. He laughs as Deluca knocks him on the shoulder, and Roman laughs hysterically. Telling me it was a perverted joke if those are their reactions.

"Well, I say lets head into the dorms. Time to start our final year here before we take over for the 'rents." Leo puts out the cigarette he was puffing away on, picks up his backpack from the ground, shrugging it over one shoulder.

He and Deluca walk off, as Tibs gives me one final look. I walk past him, hitting his shoulder in the process. Roman catches up with me. Even though I have my back facing him, I am on high alert. Tiberius is cooking something up, what it is I haven't a clue, but I'll make sure to be three steps ahead of him.

Chapter 12

Annabeth

A I managed to find my way to the main office by myself, everyone in this room looks at me as though I have two heads. Some look away from me the moment my eyes land on them. This place gets weirder and creepier the longer I stand here looking around.

"Can I help you deary?" An older woman with greyish hair is looking at me from over top her desk. She has her glasses down to the middle of her nose. Taking a closer look I can see her eyes are a deep brown color.

I give her a small smile, as I walk up to her desk, ignoring all others in the room. "Yes, hello, I'm new here and wondering where my dorm room is, and I need to pick up my class schedule." I worry about how this year will be for me, and bite down on my bottom lip, as she types something into the computer.

"Oh yes, here you are. Annabeth, correct?" She looks up at me with her eyebrows raised. I simply nod my head.

"Okay deary, my name is Mrs. Winnifred. I work in the office here in the morning and am also the history professor here." She gives me a warm smile, as she taps one of the keys on her keyboard. A second later she stands from her chair and is off retrieving a paper from the printer.

"Here is your class schedule deary, now if you'll follow me, I'll lead you to tower B. That is where you'll be residing with the others." She announces the last word with a bit of disdain in her voice. Making me wonder if there is something I have missed?

I'm too nervous to ask any questions, so I remain silent as she leads me through the halls. We go through so many doors, and different hallways, I hope I can find my way to my room and classes on my own. Finally, we make it to a dingy wooden door, when she opens it the hinges creak like it hasn't been cleaned in years.

She waves me into the room with her hand and looks at me with annoyance. "This is your stop deary." She says to me with a tight smile on her lips. Slowly, I walk into the quarters, looking around I see cobwebs in the corner of the room, with a giant brick fireplace on the far end, with couches and chairs placed randomly around the large room.

"This is the living quarters, everyone in your tower shares this area, the bathroom, and the kitchen. Then you have a room in which you share with one person." Mrs. Winnifred explains as she walks around the room, pointing things out as she speaks to me.

"In here as you can see is the kitchen, you get an allowance every other week. Where you can go to the store on campus and pick up a few necessities that you'll need throughout the month."

"Oh, thought I heard voices." I hear a high-pitched girly voice say from behind us. Turning around I can see a girl about my age, with golden hair down to her shoulders, deep brown eyes, over some bushy eyebrows, and thin lips. If she would do something with her hair and eyebrows, she'd be even prettier in appearance.

Judging by the looks of her baggy clothes she tries to hide in plain sight. I can already tell from that little bit of information that alone we may be good friends.

"Miss McKenzie, this here is Annabeth. She's the newest edition to our school here." Mrs. Winnifred waves her hand practically in my face.

"Annabeth I'd like you to meet Louisa McKenzie. She will take things from here with showing you around. I have things to do, and she just happens to be your roommate." I watch with wide eyes, as the old woman turns around and walks out the door. Slamming it behind her.

"She seems lovely." I whisper with a hint of sarcasm plaguing my tone. A burst of laughter catches my attention.

"You have no idea." I look over at Louisa, she's shaking her head looking at the now closed door.

"I'm sorry where are my manners. Hi, as she told you I'm Louisa. I'm sixteen and on most days can find me here in our quarters lounging around." She gives me a bright smile.

Her positive attitude is contagious, within seconds I'm feeling more at ease and smiling myself. "Annabeth," I point to my chest.

"So, you are my roommate?" She nods her head in affirmation, as she takes my hand and leads me to the stairs.

"Sure am. There aren't too many of us in this tower. There's a total of ten of us, well now eleven since you have come along." She smiles back at me as she leads me through the hallway to our bedroom door.

When she opens it, I take a look into the room. It's decent size, with two twin beds. One on each side of the room, a couch in the center, two closet doors, and a desk for each of us in the corners of the room.

"The left side is yours, hope you don't mind but I need to sleep on this side. It's an abnormal necessity I have." She tells me as she jumps onto her neatly made pink bed. Her entire side is made up of the color pink. No need to ask what her favorite color is.

"I don't mind at all." I say with the close of the door behind me.

Ezekiel

Roman and I make our way to our dorm in Tower A. It's the nicest tower in the entire school. It has its own cappuccino machine, regular coffee machine, and many soda machines throughout the halls of the tower. It's the biggest living quarters, filled with a sixty-inch flat screen above the nicely built fireplace. There are about six couches, a love seat, and two chairs that make up the seating in the room.

The kitchen in our tower, has a pearly white island in the center. A wrap around counter space, with multiple cupboards. There's a big farmers sink, and a refrigerator that talks to you. One where you can talk to it, and it'll make a list of things you need to remember, play your favorite music, or simply allow you to play games on it.

Our room that we share, is twice the size of anyone else's. The walls are blue, and it is made up of two king size beds on each side. Two desks in each corner, a wrap around couch in the center of the room, and another flat screen television above our very own fireplace. I drop my bag along the floor and throw myself on top of my bed. Closing my eyes, I enjoy the silence of our room for a moment.

"Senior year finally! I'm going to get so much pussy this year. I have it all planned out." Roman's words cause a knowing smile to form on my lips.

The jackass says that every year. Don't get me wrong he sure gets plenty of ass, but it's not nearly as much as he claims. He tries to come off as an asshole, one that plays with girls hearts and breaks them in his wake. The truth is he cares how he treats them. Winds up being with a girl for weeks at a time, before they mutually have enough of one another, and they move on to the next.

It's the same every year. I humor him though, "Of course bro. You'll get plenty of pussy this year. I can't wait to hear the numbers at the end of the year."

He laughs at my words. "You know it. I would say let's have a competition like we usually do, but..." He pauses causing me to open an eye and seeking him out. Lifting my body up, I lean against the pillow.

"But what Roman?" My voice comes out in a deadly whisper.

My best friend simply shrugs his shoulders, with a shake of his head. "I think we both know there's only one young lady that has your attention. Pretty sure she's going to be the only one that you play with this year."

He laughs as a loud growl works its way up my throat. I hate to admit it to the asshole, but my wolf is nodding his head and licking his chops at the idea of playing with the little human.

He's not wrong. She's ours! I hear him say inside my head as he begins pacing around.

"Shut the fuck up." I say out loud, causing Roman to laugh so hard he ends up bent over holding his stomach.

"You talking to me or your wolf?" The asshat has the audacity to raise a brow at me as he asks that question.

I blow him off, by making my way to the bathroom. Slamming the door in his face, may be an immature thing to do, but it makes me feel a little better. Looking in the mirror at my reflection I can see my eyes are a bright golden color. Just thinking about Annabeth has me hot and bothered.

"Fuck!" I holler out loud, as I strip off my clothes and decide to take a cold shower. Otherwise, I may go out and hunt for the delectable little human I can't get out of my head.

Chapter 13

E zekiel

It's been three days, and I have found myself each one of those days watching Annabeth. The school placed her in tower B, turns out my father wanted her to be close to me in case anyone tries to give her any problems. I find I am both grateful and pissed off at the knowledge. Every night I tell Roman I am going for a run to let off some steam, really, I am right outside her window waiting for the light to turn off.

Once it does, I wait ten minutes, before I climb up the side of the wall, opening her window, I let myself in to watch her sleep. Her roommate woke up the first night, eyes wide looking over to the side at me. I know she wanted to ask me what I was doing in their room but knowing who I am she thought better of it and turned her body around so she couldn't see me.

I hate myself as I find I cannot keep my hands off of her. No matter how hard I try, I still find myself at her bedside, removing her hair from her face, and lightly dragging my fingers down her arm. I allow myself to stay all of twenty minutes, until I feel I may not be able to control myself a moment longer. I jump out the window, landing on my feet. As I look up, I see the window being closed behind me. Then I go for a run.

After that first night, I waited outside of the first class we had, for that pathetic half human, half witch roommate of Annabeth's. I blocked her exit, after everyone left the classroom. Glaring down at her, she wouldn't meet my eyes. She simply looked to the side where my arm was hanging from the door.

"I won't say a word." That's all I wanted to hear her say. Without a backward glance I walked away, trusting she will keep her mouth shut.

Tiberius has been hanging around the little human at lunch time. Purposely, waiting to hit the lunch line until she comes down the hall. I'm not liking it one bit, and he knows it. He swaggers over to our two tables in the back, it's where all the elite sits. The ones that come from the most powerful witch and werewolf families. He's at least smart enough to sit at the furthest spot from me. Otherwise, I may just be tempted to knock his head from his shoulders.

Today, I find I'm more antsy than normal. Everyone and everything are pissing me off beyond belief. I know I'm being a flat-out asshole today. I just don't understand why. When I catch Annabeth out of the corner of my eye, wearing that little skirt that falls just above her knees, with a light blue tight shirt on, suddenly it comes to me.

I make my way across the hall to where she stands by the girls' locker room. Taking a hold of her arm, I drag her behind me into that room. There are about five other females here in the room, but once they see me, they clear out quite fast.

"What is your problem?" I wait until I hear the door close behind the last girl leaving, before I pull her in front of me.

Walking her backwards, I wait for her back to hit the locker, before raising my arms and caging her in. I lean my body into hers, causing her head to tilt back so she can look up at me. I bring my face right into her hair, smelling her natural smell with a hint of cherry blossom. It's her signature scent, I realized this the first night we met.

I can feel her chest rising and falling faster, as my proximity is making her both nervous and aroused.

Bringing my lips close to her ear, I ask "What the fuck are you wearing?"

Her entire body freezes beneath mine. I know she's pissed off at my question, but I don't give a damn. She shouldn't be wearing something this revealing in front of a bunch of hormonal werewolves. It's hard enough for us to keep our cocks in our pants without a woman flaunting her body our way.

Annabeth

How dare he ask me that question! It's none of his fucking business what I wear and when. I shove at his chest, but the overgrown butthead refuses to budge. Deciding he isn't going to move until he wants to, I just drop my arms as I tell him about my thoughts on the matter.

"Not that it's any of your business, but it's the weekend. I don't need to wear the school uniform, so I thought I would dress comfortably."

I know I let some of my sassy bitch out in my tone, but when I'm around him I can't help it. He brings my bitchy side out. The only person I find that brings this side of me out.

He finally pulls back, bringing his face an inch in front of mine. He's so close I can see his nostrils flare at my tone. I know he hates that I am not afraid of him, although there is a huge part of me that says I should be. However, fear isn't the first emotion I feel when he's around. That would be arousal, lust, and need.

The second thing I know for certain is he wouldn't harm me in a physical way. Everyone has told me to be very afraid of him, just to place my head down, and walk as fast as I can in the opposite direction when him and his friends are around. Call me stupid but I face him head on and give him all the attitude I can.

Judging by the look in his eyes, the dilation of his pupils. He loves that I challenge him. At least, I can feel a big part of his body does. Although, judging by the pinch of his lips, and the tension in his jaw there's a part of him that wants to kill me right now. I blatantly refuse to back down, I lift my head, bring my shoulders back, and glare at him head on.

His eyes are looking all over me. I can see clearly as day the war going on in his head. It's the same one I'm fighting on a daily basis myself. We both hear the door open; he moves his body in front of me and looks over his shoulder. I hear that bitch Jizelle say a half assed sorry as she turns on her heal and walks out of the room.

When he looks back at me, our lips are a millimeter apart. I hear a growl in the back of his throat before I see the decision made in his eyes looking back at me. His hands reach for my head, on both sides, as his lips come crashing down on mine. Thank goodness for his body being right in front of me, holding me up. I'm afraid I would have fallen to my knees with how hot this kiss is if he wasn't.

Chapter 14

E <u>zekiel</u>

I was going to only give her a warning, perhaps scare her a little into changing. Those ideas went out the fucking window the moment I touched her. With her body this close to me, I find I cannot help myself. I need to touch her, to have my lips on her. There's a big part of my body that wants to be inside of her, but I chastise him on a daily basis since meeting her.

I can't want a human in this way, let alone want to fuck her. I'm afraid I may hurt her severely if I try. Which is another thing that pisses me off about this woman. She makes me care about her. I feel for her, think about her, want to know what she is thinking about all the time, and I don't want to see her cry again. Normally, I don't give a fuck about anyone.

The more they cry and are upset the better. Just means they know how much of an asshole I am and will stay far away. It's safe to say I am not a people person. I hate most people, werewolf, witches, and humans alike. As I lick my tongue into her mouth, battling against hers I know there is something more to this girl.

The moment her leg wraps around me, her mound right where I need it, and her hands in my hair pulling on the strands all thoughts leave my head. As my blood makes its way further down my body. Once her lower region begins rubbing against me, I know I have to put a stop to this. I pull away from her sensational lips, reach for her arms behind my head, and crash them against the lockers behind her.

She doesn't flinch, not once. Any other person that knows me would be afraid right now, but I don't smell fear on her. All I can smell is a new set of determination, and a whole lot of desire. A salacious smile forms on my lips when I think of how kinky this little human must be. The more forceful I am with her, the more I smell her sweet honey.

I move my head to just a millimeter away from her mouth once more, "Something tells me, you, little one like it rough."

Her breathing picks up speed, as I look down at her neck, I see the spot where her heartbeat is moving clear as day. She's both excited and turned on.

"You don't want me little one, I'll break you beyond repair." I don't know where that came from, but it actually hurts my heart knowing how true my words are.

She looks up at me, with a fierce look behind her eyes. She moves that little bit to kiss my lips. I try to deepen it, but she pulls back, looking up at me she tells me something I never thought I'd hear from a little weakling like her.

"I know I can handle what you have to give." She looks from my lips and back up to my eyes.

"I know for a fact that you can't."

My mind is trying to push her far away from me, but my body is doing everything to keep her close. The moment I feel her leg begin to fall from my waist, I reach behind me and stop her movement. I lift it higher, as I rub myself along her center. She closes her eyes for a moment, her hands dropping to my shoulders.

Her nails dig into my skin, driving me crazy with a need I have never had for another. When she opens her eyes, she glares up at me.

"Why don't you let me make my own decisions?" Her question stuns me still. She takes the moment to drop her leg from my body, pushing me away from her, she dives under my arms and makes her way to the door.

Before she turns to go down the hall leading to the exit she freezes in place. I know she's having a war with herself, just as much as I am. Turning around she storms back to me, with a newfound determination in her eyes.

"I'm not sure what your deal is. You talk down to me like I am below you, you degrade me every moment you can, but at the same time you can't keep your hands or lips off of me." She walks right into my body, for once causing me to walk backward.

"You warn me away from you but keep making these moments where we are alone." She pokes my chest with her finger for emphasis.

"You say I make you crazy, that I'm a 'little one', whatever the hell that means," She continues on her lecture as my back hits the wall. Looking up at me, she doesn't back down, she is a woman on a mission.

"So, here's the deal, until you can at least talk to me with a little bit of the respect I deserve and stop acting like a complete asshole towards me. Your hands and lips are no longer allowed to touch me."

She places her hands on the side of my body, "You are top dog here, I get that. Everyone is either afraid of you, craves you, or worships the ground your feet walk on. I've realized that the week I have been here, but I am not one of your subordinates."

Her arms drop from the wall, as she crosses them over her chest. Making my eyes drop down. I can't help but to lick my lips at the sight before me. I know It's completely the wrong time, but the pissed off look on her is hotter than hell.

She snaps her fingers in front of my face and lifts my chin with her finger.

"My eyes are up here. That is the only thing you will have the pleasure of seeing for a while, or ever if your attitude does not change." I reach out for her arm, but just before my hand makes contact, I see a bit of gold fill the irises of her eyes. Stopping my movement all together.

She steps back from me, "What is wrong with you?"
She studies me for a moment, her head tilted to the side.

"Zeek, you look like you've seen a ghost." Her demeanor has changed immensely, but I pay that no mind. My thoughts are on her eyes changing color. To the golden color none the less. Only one species in our world has their eyes do that with strong emotions. I briefly see her shake her head before she mutters a few choice words below her breath.

"I have to go. Catch you later when you can actually have a decent conversation." She walks away from me.

The confusion I'm feeling doesn't take away from the sight of her backside walking away from me. If what I'm thinking is true, she is more than human as I have believed since the moment, I laid my eyes on her. I have plans for that ass of hers here soon. First, I crack my neck and walk out of the girl's locker room. With a newfound determination to find out everything I can about this girl that fascinates me to no end.

Chapter 15

Annabeth

To say this elite school for the privileged is strange, is right on the mark if I do say so myself. I sit in the big classrooms, that seem more for a college with the way they are set up. The chairs are all up above, in a circular form. The rows going down towards the floor, where at the center is the long table, the teacher uses for a desk.

There are strange books, with weird markings on a few of the tables that I can see. Once the teacher sees me eyeing them however, they move them into a drawer or on the bookshelf. When they speak about certain things, they use words such as 'gift', or 'things you were blessed with at birth.' Looking around the room, no one else looks confused. I stand alone with that as usual.

It says on the schedule that the lessons are supposed to last about an hour and a half, but about forty-five minutes in the teacher dismisses me. Louisa gives me one of her bright smiles when I look at her with confusion.

Nodding her head to the door, she whispers to me "We will catch up a little later on and maybe watch a movie." As though it's not strange in the least.

There is something more going on here, and I know Arthur said that he is part of an elite religion, but I have yet to hear anyone discuss anything on the subject. If anything, with the way some of my peers are dressed makes me believe he's full of shit! Looking around I see many dressed in all black, with holes in their pants, and some have piercings on their face. Every weekend they dress this way. Of course, on the school days we all have the same uniforms to wear, and apparently, they must take out their piercings while in class.

Whenever I ask Louisa about the strange occurrences that have happened, she looks away from me and quickly changes the subject. Letting me know my gut instinct is correct. I haven't seen Ezekiel all week, it's been a total of five days since my eyes have seen him or had his body close to mine. His hands touching my skin, and his lips driving me crazy.

I asked Tiberius about him yesterday in class. His jaw got tight with tension, a solemn look appearing on his face, and he leaned in his chair, cracking his knuckles. He refused to look at me the rest of class, telling me he went home for some family business. Apparently, it happens often with him. I would think his family would be more concerned with his schooling. I was always taught how important it was, but it seems to mean diddly squat to most of these people.

When Louisa walks through our bedroom door, with a book clung to her body, I feel relief. I need to talk to her desperately about what's been going through my mind. When her eyes make their way up and she sees me, they widen in shock, as she pauses mid-step.

"Oh, hey. I thought we were meeting down at the cafeteria." She looks around the room, as though someone else is here hiding and going to jump out of the closet and spook her.

"Okay," I stand from my bed, arms crossed over my chest.

"Explain to me why you're acting weird." I lift a brow at her and await to see what she says. She switches from one leg to the other, placing her hair behind her ear, she looks behind her. Out the open door, as though she's hoping someone can help her.

"Enough!" I stomp over to her, grabbing hold of her arm.

"What is everyone in this place hiding?" She looks up at me with tear in her eyes. Until a moment later it changes to the same look Ezekiel gave me five days ago.

"Your eyes..." She whispers just below her breath.

"What about them?" I ask.

She moves a few steps closer to me. Causing me to feel a bit claustrophobic in the small room. I find myself taking a step back to keep a safe distance away.

"Why does everyone keep looking at me like they've seen a ghost or something?" I whisper more to myself than her.

"First Ezekiel, now you...." Before I can finish my sentence, she cuts me off.

"Ezekiel looked at you strangely the last time you two had a confrontation?" She asks with a hint of fear coding her words.

"Yes, but he didn't say anything about my eyes. Just studied me closely like you keep trying to do." I swat her away when she moves closer to me once more.

"Sorry," she takes a step back, shaking her head, she moves to her bed. Sitting upon it, she looks like she's in a daze.

"I just can't believe this." She says more to herself than me once more.

Walking to my bed, that is a few feet away from her, I sit down, placing my elbows on top of my knees. Steepling my fingers I wait for her to acknowledge me.

"I can't tell you anything. The entire teacher staff and students have been sworn to not say a word to you." Her words make my heart speed up a beat.

"What are you talking about? You're not making any sense." I wave both hands in the air in frustration.

"If I'm being completely honest, you're sounding a little too ominous for my liking." She gives me a sad smile before she looks down at the book that is placed on her lap.

When I look down, I see the intricate design on the cover. "What is that?" This time she doesn't hide it from me, like she normally would.

Instead, she runs her fingers over the design with a smile on her face. "One of the many secrets of this place." She says as she looks up at me.

This is the first time she hasn't brushed my thoughts aside or tried to change the subject. She actually admitted this place has secrets. Many of them according to her.

"What secrets?" I watch her closely. She doesn't stop her finger tracing, but she will no longer look at me.

"I can't tell you." Her voice comes out in a whisper.

I want to open my mouth to beg her, possibly even guilt her about how friends don't keep secrets from one another, but when her eyes come to me, they stop me in my tracks. The tears let me know she already feels guilty about it.

"Ask Ezekiel. He is the only one that can tell you anything."

"Why?" I ask confused. She shrugs her shoulders and wipes away her tears.

"Because of whom he is." I stand from the bed and pace the floor in front of her.

"I would if I could. I haven't seen him here all week, and I really do not want to go back to where Arthur and my mom are." I nibble my lip, trying to figure out what I can do.

"Umm, Annabeth..." I stop my pacing and look at her.

"He's back. You can find him in the cafeteria."

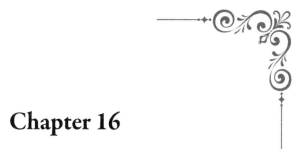

Chapter 16

E zekiel
 <u>**Five Days Earlier...**</u>
Once my new obsession is out of my sight, I make my way to my vehicle. I make sure to go the back way and use the underground tunnels. That way no one will bother the hell out of me. I have no time to talk, or with all the little female witches and Were's time to listen as they blubber on about some nonsense.

Nope, I don't have time for anything, other than getting home and demanding my mother and father tell me everything they know. I should have known something was up with this. I know they try to keep Arthur as tame as they can by giving him what he wants usually but giving him permission to marry a human female I couldn't comprehend.

Now it's all starting to make sense. There is something more to her daughter, although judging by the way they have nothing in common with one another. Not in the looks department, or facial expressions, nor their body language. Something tells me that isn't her real mother. Either way I'm going to find out tonight.

I place my car in reverse and squeal my tires the entire length of the underground garage. Only the higher and more powerful family bloodlines are allowed to park down here. The guards must be able to tell I'm in no mood to talk or discuss things. They simply open the gate and watch as I speed out of the cave.

Normally, I take my sweet time on the ride back to the estate. Anything to make the trip drag on I do. Whether its stopping for gas, pulling over to take a piss, or being an asshole and slowing down on purpose to piss off whoever is behind me.

Not today! I'm going well over the speed limit, as I fly by, not stopping at any stop signs or red lights. Briefly, I hear people honk their horns at me as I speed on by them. I pay them no mind, nothing matters to me right now but getting the truth.

Within an hour, I pull up outside of the estate. My father's men don't waste anytime opening the iron gate for me, and I speed on up right to the front door. I waste no time putting the car in park, pulling the keys out of the ignition, and hopping out. Taking the steps two at a time, another man pulls open the door for me.

"Father!" I holler out into the extravagant room, hearing the sound of my voice echo off the pristine white walls and tall ceilings. Wasting no time, I walk through the ornate halls, down some stairs, opening all the doors, looking for the man I hate with a passion.

"He isn't here darling." The sound of my mother's voice behind me has me turning around.

She's leaning her shoulder against the wall, her head tilted to the side as she squints at me. Studying her, I can see she's got a scotch in one hand, and her phone in the other.

"Mother, have you been drinking all day?" I ask while walking closer to her. She lets out a giggle, one that I have heard time and time again. It has no joy in the sound, it holds more of misery.

"Why do you ask me that darling? You clearly know the answer." She pats my cheek with her hand holding the cell phone, I think she forgot it was there.

"Where is he?" I try to keep my voice neutral, but I fail miserably. She drops her hand from my face, taking a sip of her drink, as she turns her body to slide down the wall.

"Where do you think? He's with one of his many whores." She snorts below her breath. I am anything but amused. My parents have been like this my entire life. Everyone knows in our world you seldom marry for love, it's more all about power, but my mother was in love once. Apparently, her father made an agreement with my father's, and she tried to run away with the love of her life. Needless to say, it didn't go well. She never got her happy ever after.

If she wasn't a werewolf, I'm positive she would kill herself, but unfortunately for her our kind heals quickly. Meaning even if she tried it wouldn't do her any good. I slide down to the floor, leaning my head back against the wall, enjoying the quiet and solitude of our home. If you can even call it that.

"You found out, didn't you?" Her voice whispered in my ear has my eyes popping open, and my head turning in her direction.

I must look as confused as I am because she clarifies. "About the little human girl." She takes another sip of her drink. Her words have my attention. I turn my body to face her, knowing good and well she is drunk enough to give me everything I want to know.

"Well, she isn't really human at all." She laughs under her breath.

"That's why your dear old daddy allowed Arthur to marry her mother. To get Annabeth under his control." She looks at me out of the corner of her eye. Licking my lips, I give her a nod to let her know I'm listening. Hoping she will go on with more information.

"Truth is we've been looking for her for many years. She's the last of them." Her eyes begin drooping, as her head leans further to the side.

"Mom." I shake her shoulder, causing her eyes to open wider. Turning to face me, she drops her now empty glass and brings her hands to my face, "I knew the moment I met her she was yours." She taps my cheek with her fingers, giving me a watery smile on her lips.

"What do you mean mother?" I ask below my breath, knowing full well when her head hits my shoulder that she isn't awake any longer. I lay my head on top of hers, awaiting for the man whore who is my father to come home. So, he can take her to bed, and we can have a nice chat about things.

Present Day

I sit back in my chair at the cafeteria table, watching everyone as they walk by me. Nodding my head every time someone tries to gain my attention.

Deciding, I have a lot to think about, I cancel everyone out by bringing my hat down over my eyes, stretching my legs to the chair across from me, and place a quiet spell surrounding me.

Now that I can't hear a thing, I have time to work out everything my mother had said to me that day. As well as the things my father told me about little Annabeth when he returned home. A sly smile forms on my lips just thinking about it. What the girl doesn't know is she really is mine. Hell, her father, and biological mother went through great lengths to keep her away from me.

They wanted her to have a normal, human life, one where we would never meet. Meaning the mating bond wouldn't have an effect, and she would have a choice of what she really wanted in life. Too bad for them, that somehow, we found her, living with a human woman, and now she's right where she belongs.

I feel someone kick my legs from the chair, causing them to land hard on the floor. Not being in the mood to deal with anyone's shit when I'm trying to work through all this, I raise my hat from my eyes, and reverse the spell below my breath. Ready to beat the shit out of whoever did that.

However, when I see little Miss Annabeth standing there, beside the chair, her hands on her hips, and a scowl on her face, I find I can't help the conniving smile that forms along my lips. Only making her scowl more.

"I called your name a good three times. How the hell could you not hear me?" She demands.

"Speak of the devil and she shall come." I say loud enough for those around us to hear. Causing some people to laugh out loud. When she turns her head, others look away trying to hide their faces from her view. When she turns her face back to me, I can't help the blood in my body from going to one specific place. She is hot as hell when she pissed off.

Makes me want to throw her down on the floor, right here, in front of everyone and take her like I've been dying to since the first night I saw her.

"Can we please go somewhere to talk. It's important." The madness has now left her eyes, as uncertainty takes its place. When she looks around the cafeteria I understand completely. We have an audience, and she doesn't like that at all.

I say nothing, only stand from the chair and begin leaving the room. It's quiet behind me for a few seconds, but then I hear her little footfalls right behind me. I can feel everyone's eyes along our backs, but I don't give a shit what anyone is thinking about all this. Let them talk for all I care. Watching her out of the corner of my eye, I can't help but wonder if she knows who she is, and that her entire life has been one big lie?

Chapter 17

Annabeth
      I wrap my arms around my center, giving me the strength to have this discussion with him. Before I was in his presence, I had it all worked out in my head. I would charge in and demand he tell me everything! However, once his eyes were on me, looking at my body from the top of my head all the way down to my toes, I couldn't help but lose some of my bravado. The rest of it flew out the window once his eyes took on a hooded look.

I no longer was a nuisance bothering him while he was trying to sleep. No, instead his eyes were looking at me as though he would eat me if given the chance. That thought shouldn't make my heart skyrocket, or my toes curl in my shoes, but it doesn't stop my body's reaction. I hadn't realized where we were going, my eyes cast down at the ground, thinking of how I wanted to do this, when suddenly I am bumping into his back.

He whips around, his arm wrapped around my center, and it takes me a moment to realize what he's doing. When I see the light blue sky behind his head, I realize I had almost fallen back, but he caught me just in time. I'm breathing hard, being this close to him. I can see little green specks in his eyes. Studying him further I can see when he smiles, he has a dimple that shows on his cheek.

His lips are beautiful. I know that sounds weird describing them that way, but they are. They are pink, plump, and I find myself imagining biting down hard on his bottom one. He stands tall, bringing me with him. My hands land on his shoulders, as our noses touch with the excursion.

I can't help myself, my hands grab on tight to his shoulders, before working their way down to his chest. I can feel his heart beating faster as I explore him for the first time. He is just as effected by me as I am him. I hear a growl building in his throat, that sound making my thighs rub together. Trying and failing miserably to get the fire growing between my legs extinguished.

"What did you want to talk about?" His voice sounds gruff, as his arm tightens around my center. He takes a few steps backward, leaning his body against a tree. He looks down at me, his eyes hungry with need. I'm certain mine look similar as I try to shake my head to clear those thoughts away.

"Could you umm..." I look down, his eyes follow.

I feel his hand tighten behind me before his fist loosens and he releases me. Taking a few steps back, away from him, I clear my throat. Trying to work through my muddled thoughts. I turn away from him, taking a deep breath and releasing it a moment later.

"I need to know that I'm not crazy." I start with a whisper.

I hear him snort at me, whipping around I see the egotistical male with his leg behind him along the tree. A cigarette at his lips, he takes a deep drag from it, before blowing it out his nose. His head turning to the side, waiting for me to continue. When I don't, he lifts his hand in the air waving me to finish my thought.

"I know there is something more here. This isn't just 'gifted' students." I air quote with my fingers the word.

"There's more to this place isn't there?"

As my words fall from my lips, the breeze picks up. My hair blowing in my face, I pull my sweater tighter around me. Looking up at the sky I can see grey clouds forming above us. It makes no sense. It was just clear skies, sunny, and warm only moments before.

"You certain you want the answer to that," I hear him whisper in my ear, causing me to jump back.

I hadn't realized he moved close to me I was so distracted. I watch in a trance as he throws his cancer stick down to the ground, stomping it out. I can see he's licking his teeth behind his closed mouth.

Sweeping his eyes up and down my body, he brings his thumb to his lips and rubs his bottom lip. A moment later, he looks directly into my eyes. His once blue green eyes are now pure gold. The change causes me to stumble backwards. This time he lets me fall, my ass hitting the hard ground. I wince in pain, but don't remove my eyes from his.

He laughs at me, "I think the real question you should be asking yourself is who the hell you are?" He bends down so he's eye level with me once more.

Bringing his hand close to my face, he rubs his finger along my tightly closed lips, down my chin, and I feel them disappear below my sweater.

"Well, I suppose I should say what you are." He shrugs his shoulders. As though everything he is saying right now makes sense.

Deciding there is a good chance this man kneeling in front of me is crazy, I scramble back, lifting myself up with my hands along the ground. Wiping them clean, I turn to face him, realizing my mistake a second later. The school is behind him, meaning the only thing behind me at the moment is the forest.

He laughs, the sound holds no joy, only a sadistic sound to it, that brings real fear to my bones. I'm shaking where I stand, I watch in curiosity and fascination, as he lifts his head, closes his eyes, and takes a deep breath of the air surrounding us. I'm stunned when he opens his eyes, instead of saying a word, he simply lifts his shirt up over his head.

I take a step back, not removing my eyes from the confusing man before me. With a devious smile he unbuttons his pants and brings his zipper down. *Is he going to do bad things to me now?* There's a pulse between my legs that shouldn't be there at that thought. No! I should be horrified at the idea.

"I'm not going to do anything that won't excite you at your core." He answers my silent question.

Taking another step back, I hear the snap of a branch. We both stop where we stand, frozen, looking at one another.

"You may want to run little human." I don't have time to think about what he called me. I only turn away and run through the trees, my heart beating faster and faster as I push myself further along.

The sound of a dog howling has me looking behind me for a moment. The rustle of branches, and twigs snapping behind me has me picking up the pace. I knew there was something more to the people here.

More behind the grungy walls and fake smiles from the people of this school. Now, I'm about to get my answers, and a big part of me thinks I should have just been left in the dark.

Chapter 18

E<u>zekiel</u>
   I run through the woods in my wolf form. Chasing after the most magnificent prey I have ever had in my life. I know I could have simply explained to her there outside of the school what we are. About all the secrets of the school, but what would be the fun in that? I see her sweet ass, through those tight jeans she has on, as she runs. Her face keeps turning around to see what's exactly chasing her.

When we come up to a brush of trees she jumps through, me right behind her. When I land on all fours, looking up I see a clear space, not a tree in sight. She isn't running, simply standing there, her shoulders folded in, trying to catch her breath. Frantically, she looks around the area, looking for any place to hide.

I sit my ass on the ground wagging my tail, waiting to see what she does. She looks behind her, eyes wide, her mouth falls open. I think she wants to scream, but no noise will come out. I know she cannot believe what she's seeing.

I tilt my head to the side, studying her. Closing her eyes, I can see her lips move as she counts before opening them up once more. Within seconds she's turning back around and fleeing.

Where she thinks she's going I haven't a clue. I decide to be nice, counting to five before I run after her.

Am I playing with her? Most definitely.

Does this make me a major asshole? Absolutely!

Do I care? Fuck no.

The smell of blood in the air has me picking up my speed. Judging by how she's limping I would say she cut her foot on something.

As she runs further up, I can smell the scent of water, as well as hear the sound of it running along. Looking down, I see she's wearing flip-flops. I hadn't noticed before as my mind was elsewhere.

She must have cut her foot on a rock, and judging by the body of water up ahead, there's about to be a lot more on the ground. Deciding I have pushed her far enough, I pick up my pace, standing on my hind legs, I lunge for her.

She goes down, but I change into my human form, to wrap my arms around her. Making sure she doesn't get hurt worse than she already is. We roll along the ground a couple of times, until finally stopping completely along the mud and little bit of grass on the ground. I hold the back of her head, so her face is buried into my neck.

Her breathing is erratic, her heartbeat going well over one hundred beats a minute. I know I need to calm her down. I wouldn't want her passing out from fear.

"Hey, you're okay. I won't hurt you Annabeth. I would never hurt you." I pet her hair trying to keep my voice calm. The smell of her salty tears hits me like a truck.

Closing my eyes, I bring my nose to her hair and smell her essence. She smells like cherry blossoms and fresh air. There is a hint of something else, something powerful. That thought has a growl working its way up my throat.

Her parents did everything to keep her from our world. In turn, keeping her far away from me. If it wasn't for them, we could have grown up together. I could have taught her everything I know.

Instead, she's so far behind, and doesn't even know who she really is. That thought breaks my heart. Pulling up and away from her, she keeps her eyes closed. Allowing her tears to fall. I lean on my elbows and bring my thumbs to her face to wipe them away.

"Annabeth, look at me." She shakes her head at me, trying to pull her face away from my reach. I won't allow it.

In fact, her not listening to me and obeying me really pisses me off. I place some Alpha in my tone, and it works wonderfully. Her icy blue eyes pop open, looking like the blue sky after it rains.

"You're so beautiful little lamb." I didn't mean to say that out loud, but it's too late. She heard me loud and clear.

"Don't." She tries to close her eyes again, but I shake her head.

"No. None of that. You always look at me. Don't hide away from me. Ever!"

She looks me dead in the eye, sticking her chin out at me, giving me some of that sass I have grown to love. I bring my lips down close to hers. So, close I can feel her breath on my mouth.

"What were you going to say little lamb?" She pinches her lips tightly together. Doing everything she can to be disobedient.

Looking down, at her chest, I lick my lips and shake my head. A devious laugh falling from my lips.

"Oh, baby girl," I look up at her through my little bit of hair that has fallen into my eyes.

"You have no idea what you're doing to me." I say in a hushed tone.

I feel her heart speed up once more at my words. As well as smell the sweet scent of her honey between her legs. She licks her lips, my eyes following the motion.

"I was going to say don't lie to me."

My brows furrow with confusion for a moment. Lie to her about what? Then it hits me, why she wears the baggy clothes, pulls her hair in front of her face all the time, and humps her shoulders. She is trying to hide herself, thinking she isn't beautiful. That she's nothing special. It pisses me off!

I hold her chin between my thumb and finger.

"Let's get something straight right here and now little lamb. You are the most beautiful woman I have ever seen in my life." She rolls her eyes before she can stop it. I stand up, her eyes going to my hard cock.

"You're naked." She whispers below her breath.

I pull her up, holding onto her arm, I drag her behind me to the nearest tree.

"It happens when we change into our wolf forms. Once we return back to human, we have no clothes on." I hear her intake of breath at my words.

"This has to be some dream. A cruel joke of my wild imagination playing tricks on me." She mutters more to herself than me.

She's so transfixed on her thoughts; she hasn't realized I've placed her chest up against the tree. My body along her back, so close she couldn't escape if she tried.

"What are you doing?" She asks once she realizes the position, I have her in.

I smile against her neck, leaning back I pull her hair to one side, so I can see her eyes better.

"Punishing you." Her brows furrow, as her mouth falls open.

"What," I don't let her finish her sentence before I kick her feet apart.

Stepping back, I pull her hips away from the tree, making her hands fall down the length of it.

"Stay just like this little lamb, if you move, I'll make it worse for you." I say as I rub my hand down her back, to her ass.

I can smell her fear emanating from her skin, hear the pounding of her heart. What has me closing my eyes, leaning my head back and taking a deep breath is the honey between her legs. My woman is drenched.

Chapter 19

Annabeth
    I don't know what he means by punishing me. My body seems to know though, as my legs open wider on their own, and my tummy is doing flips. I feel a deep need in my core, that spreads all the way between my legs.

"What the hell for?" I know it's the wrong words to speak. I should be moving my body away from this tree, turning to face him and tell him there is no way I will allow him to punish me in any way.

I don't do either, I stand here, arms leaning on the tree, my hips bent, and legs spread. Awaiting for his next command. Shaking my head, I laugh under my breath.

"What's so funny little lamb?" He asks, as I feel his hands rubbing up and down my ass.

"This is the weirdest dream I have ever had." I close my lips tight, realizing what I just said. Hoping he doesn't put two and two together I stand there, quiet, and unmoving.

"You have dreamt of me?" The haughty tone of his voice makes me want to turn around and slap him clear across the face. I move to do just that when I feel his body fall on top of mine.

"I wouldn't do that baby. It'll only make things worse for you." He intertwines his fingers with mine, his breath falling along the skin of my neck.

"Do what?" I go for playing coy.

There's no way he could know what I was really going to do. Is there? I feel his face move from being buried in my hair, to beside my ear. His tongue sticks out, licking the outer ring before I feel his teeth sink into my earlobe. I mean to scream, but instead a deep moan falls from my lips. It hurt of course. The sadistic thing is I liked it.

"My kinky little lamb. The things we will do together." He releases my hands and brings his down my body.

Slowly, ever so slowly. The feel of his palms on my skin actually hurts. I hate to admit it, but there is a big part of me that wants him inside of me. Here and now. I don't care who hears us, or the possibility of being seen. That excites me that much more.

"Soon. First, you have a few things to atone for." My brows furrow with confusion. As the heat of his body goes with him, I feel cold for the first time today. I hear a loud noise, before his palm slaps me on my jean covered ass.

"Ugh. What the..." I'm unable to finish my sentence, as his hand comes down once more.

He swats my cheek a few more times, before rubbing it slowly below his hand.

"Why do you wear baggy clothes?" His question throws me for a loop. He brings his head closer to my ear, the feel of his bare chest along the skin of my arm is doing strange things to my head.

"Why do you hide baby?" I love when he calls me that. *Baby.* I know I shouldn't, he probably calls all the women of this school that.

"I," my words break off.

I don't know how to answer his question. I have always worn baggy clothes, hiding in the background or in the dark. It's where I'm most comfortable. These last few days are the only time I can recall wearing tighter shirts, and jeans. I know in my soul the reason being to entice him.

I go to open my mouth, ready to spout a lie, when his finger comes up to my lips.

"Don't lie to me." His voice has grown hard.

"I will know if you do, and then there won't be any fun to have later. It'll only be punishment." His fingers fall from my lips.

I close my mouth for a moment, breathing heavily. I'm torn, I don't like to get personal with people, but I have a strange feeling that if I am not honest he will bring me to the brink of orgasm, but won't let me get there. That thought brings sadness to my core, I find myself opening my mouth telling him the truth.

"I don't feel I am beautiful enough. I'm just plain, ordinary, well me." I shrug my shoulders.

I hear him give off a mean grunt below his breath.

"Well, let me show you what I think of that." He whispers in my air, as his other hand comes down hard on my ass. He swats me a few times, before I feel the muscles in his body tense up.

"Fuck it." He twirls me around, catching me by both arms, so I don't fall headfirst into the ground.

The next moment, his lips are on mine. This isn't like any other kiss he's given me. This is hard and holds so much passion that if he wasn't holding onto me, I'd fall to my knees. It's a punishment for my thoughts. He bites down on my bottom lip, causing me to cry out. He swallows my pain, brushing his tongue deep into my mouth. Feeding me the elixir that is merely him. With a hint of an iron taste. My blood.

The taste of it on his tongue, causes him to get more animalistic. He lifts my body up with both hands on my ass, slamming my back against the tree. One of his hands works its way up my body, before reaching my chin. He holds my face still for his onslaught.

"You taste too fucking good." He groans into my mouth.

He brings his hips close to mine, holding my body up against the tree, as his other hand makes its way to my sweater. With a growl, he takes both hands, tears my shirt completely open. Both parts of my garment drop to the ground. He pauses, once he feels my bare chest, to look down.

"No bra?" It's a question, though sounds more like a proclamation.

"I was in a hurry and forgot to put one on." I nibble my lip, as his eyes look up at me.

With a sly smirk he bends his head down, not breaking eye contact, sucking my nipple into his mouth. I moan, as my hips begin to move with the sensation coursing through my body. I have never in my life had this feeling before. I don't know what it is, but I do know I never want it to end.

He attacks my breasts, just as aggressively as he did my mouth. Taking almost the whole thing into his mouth. He sucks, licks, and bites the area, before lifting his mouth from it with a pop. Looking down, he rubs my hardened nipple with his thumb. My hands fall to his shoulders, as I ride out the waves.

Chapter 20

E zekiel
     I shouldn't be doing this with her. Especially, since there is a lot we need to discuss, but she's so beautiful. So, addictive I just need this little bit of time with her. To feel her body, undulate beneath me. To hear her soft moans, and the sound of my name all breathy as she screams it for the whole world to hear.

"Tell me to stop." I beg her because if she doesn't, I'm going to taste every part of her body I can get my mouth on.

> Here and now. She sucks her bottom lip into her mouth, her hands going from my shoulders to my pecks. She raises her eyebrows, asking for permission with those sultry eyes of hers. Deciding it's too late for her anyway, I nod my head at her. Allowing her to touch my entire upper body. The sweat from the run earlier caused her hands to slip.

I can't help but hope that she meant to do that all along. Without another thought my hands fall back to her body, looking deep in her eyes, I unbutton and pull the zipper of her jeans down. Pulling them from her body, once they reach her knees, I decide to keep them there. Not trusting myself, to have complete access to her body.

I may lose control and take her here and now. She isn't ready for that. I'll know when she is and believe me when I say I won't hold myself back. I drop to my knees in front of her.

> "Place your hands along top my shoulders and do not move them." I demand her.

She does as I tell her, but she can't help herself. My innocent minx looks down at me, with mischief in her eyes.

"If I do?" I give her a sly smirk before I bend down to bite the skin along her knee. She gives off a surprised holler, as she hits my shoulder with the palm of her hand.

When I look back up at her, I tell her again.

"Keep them there." She must know how serious my warning is.

She nods her head, giving me the submission, I crave from her. I have never once felt like a dominant male in a sexual manner. Normally, it's taking them from behind, just to get there so I can have a small release from stress.

With her, it's different, I want to control her. I want all her firsts, to make her cry out in pain, then to take care of her after. It's a cluster fuck of feelings when I'm around her. I pull her silk panties down her legs, joining at her knees with her tight jeans she had around this sweet ass of hers.
"Hands." I demand as I feel her fingers in my hair.

She practically slams them back down, making a devilish smile form on my lips. I move close to her pussy, smelling her essence.

On a groan I ask, "Anyone ever tasted this pretty pussy of yours?" I wait for her answer, bringing my nose just between her wet folds. Enjoying the quiver of her legs.

When she doesn't answer me, I look up at her, seeing her cheeks as red as her hair. She looks down at me, shaking her head lightly.

"Answer me verbally Annabeth." I watch as her tongue comes out wetting her lips.

"No." When I lift an eyebrow at her, she goes on.

"I haven't done anything with anyone ever."

She looks down at the ground and away from me. It pisses me off! I stand at my full height, taking her chin in my hand I move her eyes back to me.

"Don't ever look away from me." She swallows down her fear and relaxes her shoulders. Once I am satisfied, I slowly fall to my knees once more, licking down her body as I do.

She's panting now, her chest moving fast with the excursion. Little moans falling from her lips.

"Watch as I enjoy my new favorite treat." Her mouth falls open at my words. Knowing she's watching I bring my eyes to her pretty petals in front of me. I open them up, licking into her with the precision of the werewolf I am. I hold both hips with my hands, holding her still so she can feel all the pleasure I give her.

"You're like me." I whisper against her pussy.

Her hands tighten their hold on my shoulders. I look up at her, kissing her pussy like I have her mouth many times within the last week.

"What?" Her word breaks as I continue my onslaught with my tongue.

"You are half werewolf and half witch." I suck her clit into my mouth, making her scream out in ecstasy.

Looking up at her, I move away from her pussy, kissing up her body as I stand over her. The feel of her juices along my lips and chin making me harder than stone.

"Just like me." I whisper along her lips, staring deep into her eyes. Her eyes look from one of mine to the other. She feels confused, conflicted, and lost.

Everything she is feeling I can read from those beautiful eyes of hers. Tears build behind them, causing me to clash my lips to hers once more. As they begin to fall, I open her mouth with my tongue and slide in. I want to be here for her, talk her through all of this. Comfort her, but If I'm being honest I don't know how.

All I have ever been is rough with another being, it's how I was raised. I don't know how to do sweet. Which is another reason why I could understand why her parents had done what they did. To keep her far away from our kind, out of our world. Hidden from me. When I pull back, I place my forehead along hers.

Standing close to her, giving her my strength as much as I can. Leaning against her, the sound of her cries breaks a part of me I thought had died a long time ago.

"You want to go to my room and talk?" She looks up at me, tear streaks on her cheeks.

She nods her head. I give her a sincere smile, as I pull her panties and jeans back up around her waist. Once she's set, I turn to look around the area where I know I left my clothing. Knowing she will follow I walk a few feet until I find the pile on the ground. Once I find my shirt, I hold it out on my finger for her.

"Put this on." She looks from my shirt to my face. I shrug my shoulders.

"I'm not a total asshole." I see her smile, as I turn around to pick up my jeans from the ground. Sliding them on, I look up at my woman once again. When I see all her glory is hidden underneath my shirt, I step into her once more.

"Besides no one sees what's mine." Her mouth falls open, I can see she wants to fight with me again.

I bend down and kiss her lips, shutting this infuriating woman up. When I pull away, I grab her hand and yank her close behind me. We are going to my domain. She doesn't know, but this may be another mistake on her part. With how I'm feeling I'm not so certain I'll allow her to leave my room once I have her there with me.

Chapter 21

Annabeth

I try not to let the fact that he said I was his get me too excited. He's probably said that to many girls before me. I allow him to pull me along. Me quiet and stuck in my head. He's a werewolf and male witch? To make matters worse as though that isn't a lot to wrap my head around, he says I'm just like him.

It takes us about ten minutes to reach his room, each one of those minutes my heart is beating faster and faster, as time moves on. Once we are outside the door to the wing he lives in, it bursts open before he can reach his hand out. I recognize the young man standing there, studying us with a coy smile along his lips from a few classes.

"Well, well, well, it looks as though the cat has finally given in to its cravings and caught the canary." He leans against the threshold of the door with one shoulder, his arms crossed over his chest, eyes moving between Ezekiel and me.

"Shut the fuck up Roman, or I'll make you." Ezekiel's tone is so low and sounds deadly. It has me shivering a little in fear for his friend.

I'm ashamed to admit that it makes me want to climb him like a tree. His words nor the tone of them has little to no effect on Roman. He simply tilts his head to the side, laughing below his breath.

Holding his hands out, he stands at his full height, "Hey I'm just calling it like I see it." His stares deep into Ezekiel's eyes. I feel as though they are having a private conversation I cannot hear.

After a few seconds, though it feels like hours, I see him nod his head. His eyes making their way to me, "Interesting."

He looks at my body up and down, not in a checking me out kind of way, but like he's placing all the missing pieces about me together.

When his eyes fall back to Ezekiel, he gives a genuine smile. "Interesting indeed. I can't wait to see how this plays out."

He moves back a couple steps from the door, holding his arm out behind him.

"Please won't you both come in." He bows down, as though we are royalty. Zeek rolls his eyes at him, as he places a hand along my back, allowing me to walk in first. Him close behind me.

When I hear the door close, I feel a rock at the pit of my stomach. I'm not certain why, but I feel as though I need to be cautious. Looking behind me, I can see that Roman is no longer around. Meaning Zeek and I are alone. He's leaning against the closed door to his room, one leg behind him, the other still on the floor.

He folds his arms over his chest, tilting his head to the side, he looks at my body up and down. The look in his eyes staring back at me makes me squirm on the spot. the look held in his eyes is completely different from Roman's. He is definitely looking at me as though he's hungry and I'm the dessert on the menu. Deciding I can't keep my eyes on him, I turn around and look at my new surroundings.

"Wow, this place is most definitely different from where I'm staying." I try to keep my voice from shaking.

If his laugh below his breath tells me anything, it's that I failed miserably.

"It should be," his voice a sultry whisper in my ear has me turning around. His face is an inch away from mine. I hadn't realized he moved away from the door.

"I'm going to get you a bell for around your neck. So I know when you move." I go for being funny, but he doesn't laugh at my joke.

Which causes me to take a step back, trying and failing to create distance between the two of us.

Every step back I take, he takes one forward. I know this game all too well. He's done this to me more times than I can count. I try to turn my face, to look behind me, making sure there is nothing he can back me into. My eyes don't make it, his hand whips out holding me still. Looking deep in my eyes, he walks me back a few more steps, until the cold of what feels like the counter is against my backside.

I swallow my fear and excitement. Knowing this isn't the time. Shaking my head, I force the thoughts racing through my mind out in one breath.

"How could I possibly be like you? My mother is human. Not to mention, how crazy you sound with all of this." I try to give him a coy smile, hoping he will smile back. Put my racing heart at ease.

He does no such thing. Instead that same foreboding laugh leaves his mouth. Causing my heart to drop.

"Let me put your mind at ease." His hands reach for my ass, pulling me up and placing me on top of the counter. The coldness of the tile leaks through my jeans, causing me to wiggle. Trying to get comfortable.

When I stop squirming, he brings his lips to mine for a quick kiss.

"Don't move from this spot." He tells me as he glares at me.

"I won't." My voice comes out in a breathy whisper. My emotions are everywhere.

"I mean it Annabeth. You move from this spot; I won't be able to control myself." His words have confusion setting in.

I watch him closely as he steps back away from me. Never once breaking eye contact. He unbuttons his pants, bringing the zipper down. I have to swallow the lust down and tighten my legs against each other. He knows what I'm thinking if the crude smile that forms on his lips tells me anything.

He pulls them down his muscular legs. My eyes bulging out of my head, as his cock springs out. It's so hard, long, and veiny. It reaches his belly button. I watch as his hand wraps around that part of him, rubbing his palm up and down his length.

"Hands on the counter. Grip it, so I know you won't move from that spot." He nods his head at me.

It takes me a moment, thinking about disobeying his request. That is until his voice turns deadly low.

"Do it now Annabeth." For some strange reason his words have me clutching the counter so tight my knuckles turn white.

"Good girl. Do not let go no matter what." The fear I felt earlier is building more and more with each word that falls from those plump, beautiful lips of his.

He falls to his hands and knees, my body shaking, as I hear what sounds like bones breaking. I close my eyes, not wanting to see this.

"Open them." A growl comes from in front of me.

No longer sounding like Zeek at all. When my eyes finally open, my mouth drops and I scream. Where he once stood, stands a huge black wolf. If I wasn't scared out of my mind, I would think he was beautiful.

Chapter 22

Annabeth

I forget everything he said to me earlier. Getting ready to jump down from the counter, so I can run. *Where to?* I have no idea, but I feel like an idiot if I just sit here. The wolf shakes its head at me, telling me with his eyes to stay put. I don't know why, but I do as it is telling me. I lift myself back up, on top of the counter. My entire body quivers in fear, as I try to swallow it down and look at the wolf head on.

I can practically see what he's thinking. His head tilts to the side, his long tongue coming out of his mouth to lick his chops. He stands at his full height, which is twice the size of a normal dog. Slowly, ever so slowly he prowls closer. Each step he takes has my heart beating faster. I want to run away, or better yet pretend this is just a dream.

I remember what he said, and knowing Ezekiel just turned into a large animal, one that is known to hunt, I decide to stay put. Closing my eyes, as I beg myself below my breath to wake up from this nightmare. The next moment, I feel the black beast stand on its back legs, as it places each of his front ones on either side of me.

The fur is shockingly soft against the skin of my arms. My entire body shakes more, as all the different scenarios go through my head. Some wondering what he could or wants to do to me. The others are how I'm going insane, and I'm going to wake up tethered to a bed in an asylum. Neither scenario helps me feel any better.

"Annabeth," I hear Ezekiel whisper my name as I feel the touch of his hand along my face.

Causing my eyes to pop open, I see him standing so close in front of me our noses are touching.

"I needed you to know. That what I am telling you is true." I study him for a moment longer before I jump down from the counter. Realizing how close his delectable body is to me, I instantly realize that it was a mistake on my part.

Closing my eyes, I take a few deep breaths, before I open them once more. Leaning down, I practically crawl below his arm that is caging me in and walk a few feet away. I need as much space between the two of us I can get. I begin pacing the floor, my one elbow held into the palm of my hand. My other hand on my chin, my thumb rubbing my bottom lip. I get lost in my thoughts.

That is until I hear a scoff of laughter come from where I was. Stopping my movement, I turn to face the young man that has confused me from the first moment I laid my eyes on him. Seeing him standing there, leaning against the countertop, his arms crossed over his bare chest, I have to bite my bottom lip, so I stay quiet. Otherwise, I may beg him to take me.

Especially, once my eyes make their way down his naked body. He has muscles for days, every crevice that makes up his body is beautiful. I find myself fighting the sensation to lick him from head to toe. Once my eyes make their way down past his chest, I can see the tip of his manhood below his belly button.

Quickly, I turn around. Feeling embarrassed, as I have never before seen that part of a man. I'm no expert, but he looked to be long. That part of his body pointing straight at me.

"Oh, it is," I whip back around at his words. Looking at him, wondering how the hell he knew what I was thinking?

"You spoke the words out loud." He says with a hint of humor in his tone.

Looking at his face, I can see he's trying not to laugh at my expense, but it's difficult for him. It's as though I have no real control over my eyes, as they make their way down to the center of his legs. It's not at all what I had expected. First, it's huge. *Making me wonder how the hell he fits that into a woman?* Second, I have this strange craving to lick the substance leaking from his tip.

I have to swallow that need down, not understanding where it comes from.

"If you keep looking at my cock with that innocent but wild look in your eyes," mine look back up to his as he finishes his thought. "I will not be responsible for what I do." He stands at his full height, taking one step in my direction.

I expect me to want to take one back. To do the dance we have done since the first night we've met but I don't move. I feel no fear only hunger coursing through my body. It's as though some sort of fire has been inflamed inside of me, running through my veins, and causing me to burn.

"It's because we are together." He whispers as he takes more steps my way.

He has his head bent down, his shoulders folded in. Seeming to come off as less intimidating. I raise my own head up, not knowing what is about to happen, but knowing whatever it is I won't fight him.

"There's a strong bond between you and me. It's like an inferno that was dead for the longest time." He's standing directly in front of me now.

His hand lifts to hold my chin,

"The night you showed up at the estate its as though someone poured gasoline on us, and lit a match, throwing it to set us a flame." His eyes are on mine, holding me hostage with that one look alone.

His fall following the movement of his thumb, that is rubbing my bottom lip. Back and forth, it continues on.

Without a cause, I open my mouth for him. With no hesitation he moves it along my tongue, his eyes closing at the sight in front of him.

"Suck." The word comes out more of a growl than anything.

The sound turns me into a puddle along the floor at his feet. I close my eyes, sucking his thumb like I would his tongue. He pushes it further in, so it reaches the back of my throat causing me to gag.

I find I don't mind, not one bit. I relax my throat, and allow him to move his thumb inside of my mouth. The feel of his body heat along my chest, his breath on the skin of my neck, has me moving that much closer. There isn't an inch of space between us, and for the first time I realize we are a perfect fit.

"Open those beautiful eyes of yours." He grumbles.

When I do, I see his arm moving to the side. I try to look down, but his hand holds me tightly in place, his thumb moving faster in my mouth. He brings two more fingers to my lips, telling me without any words to open my mouth once more.

When I do, he places them along my tongue too. I hear a wet sound as I feel his arm moving faster and faster. It's then I realize what he's doing. Not knowing why, but I feel like I want him to finish. There's a carnal part of me, that wants him to come all over me. He sees something in my eyes, as his widen with mirth.

A carnal smile forms on his lips, as he pulls his fingers and thumb from my mouth with a pop. Placing it along my shoulder, he helps me onto my knees in front of him.

"I'm going to finish inside your mouth," My eyes practically pop out of their sockets at his words.

Causing his smile to grow, "Then I'm going to pick you up, place you on that counter behind you, and eat you like the hungry beast I am."

I must be more of a dirty girl than I realize. His words make my thighs squirm with need. Trying and failing miserably to get the pressure I need between my legs. Without another word he places his tip along my lips. I open for him without a second thought, and he buries so deep into my throat I have tears falling from the corner of my eyes. He holds my head on each side, thrusts once, twice, and on the third I watch as his head falls back, eyes closed and a loud groan falls from those gorgeous lips of his.

"Get every drop." Are his breathy words as I feel him grow in my mouth and shoot his seed down my throat.

After the spasming of his body calms down, he keeps to his word. Before I realize what's happening, he has me up in the air. The coldness of the counter along my back, as he rips my jeans clear off my body. His head dipping between my legs.

Chapter 23

Ezekiel

I told myself I was going to bring her here to talk. Telling her everything she never knew about the world she truly belongs in. I should have known it was a lie, falling from my lips. Whenever I'm in her presence, I need to have her. At this rate, she'll have me by my balls soon enough.

Whether in the palm of her hand, licking them with her tongue, or hitting her body as I thrust into her. Either way she will have them. I feel her hands dig into my scalp, as she grabs handfuls of my hair. Pulling the strands, causing me to moan against her pussy lips. Her body shivers with the feelings I'm giving her.

"Come for me." I whisper against her little nub.

She wants to, I know this by the tightening of her muscles, but she's fighting it. I lift my head, stopping all movement. She looks at me, tears held deep in her eyes, a confused look in her eyes. She bites her bottom lip, looking away from me. I don't like it.

"No," with the authority held in that one word her eyes shoot to mine.

"You never look away from me. That's your first lesson." Her mouth falls open.

"Second lesson baby girl," I crawl up her body, slowly. Ever so slowly. Prowling like the wolf I am. Once I'm laying along the top of her body, I give her a kiss. A sweet one this time.

I pull away from her lips, with a nip of my teeth. She tries to follow my retreat, causing a knowing laugh to fall from my mouth.

"Let me take care of you." I look deep in her eyes, as I bring my hand between us, rubbing her special spot.

"Always let me take care of you." My words sound more like a growl. Letting us both know how close to the surface my wolf is.

She nods her head, as she fights to keep her eyes open and on me. She doesn't know this yet, but her trying her best to keep looking at me, will bring her great pleasure. A carnal smile forms along my lips, as I sink back down between her legs. I don't get right into my meal this time though. I take my time with her. Blowing along her sensitive skin.

Opening her beautiful petals, I look at all her substance coating them. She's wet as a tsunami, turning me on more. Licking that part of her, with just the tip of my tongue, has me going to nirvana. My head falls back, while my eyes roll into the back of my head. When I open them again, I get to work. Knowing she needs a release.

Annabeth

The things he's doing to me. What I'm allowing him to do to me, is so dirty. He just showed me his wolf self not five minutes ago, and now here I am. Sprawled on my back, legs open wide, and panting like the little hussy I apparently am.

It's as though I'm deprived little red riding hood, and I'm getting eaten out by the big bad wolf. I smile at the thought. What I really don't want anyone to know is how much more I want him to do to me. I don't even care that he, and probably everyone at this school are more than human.

All I care about is what he can do to me right now. Once I feel his tongue dip inside of me again, my legs begin to shake, my lower extremities wish to move along with his actions, but the bastard is holding me down. All I can do is feel.

"Come for me." He demands once more.

This time, I don't think. I clear my mind, allowing the sensations that he's inflicting to take hold.

The next moment I hear him holler, "Now!" That's it.

All it takes is that one powerful word coming from his mouth, and my orgasm hits me a second later. My entire body spasming with the endorphins flooding my body. I'm not certain how long my body does this, but I feel his body heat encompassing me. Opening my eyes, I see him right above me. So, close our noses are touching. Rubbing along the other.?

He smiles, not one that is carnal or devious in any way. It's a genuine smile. I can see pride held deep in his eyes. He's happy with what he did to me. How he made me feel. I want to feel embarrassed, but the feeling never comes. Instead, I bring my hand to his cheek, expecting him to turn into the asshole I know he can be.

Surprisingly, he rubs his skin along the palm of my hand. Closing his own eyes, I take this intimate moment to study him. He looks like an innocent young man right now. It has me wondering what happened to him to make him so hard?

When he opens his eyes once more, they turn serious, causing my heart to drop. Thinking he's going to be an asshole now, I snatch my hand away, bringing my other to his shoulder. I try to push him away from me. He stands up, allowing me to finally move. I use my arm to cover myself as I look for my jeans.

Once I find them, my shoulders cave in with defeat. They are completely torn down the center. There's no saving the material. He follows my line of sight, the corner of his mouth lifting.

"What can I say, I couldn't control myself any longer." He shrugs his shoulders as he speaks. The tears that have wanted to fall are back full force. I try to turn around, away from his eyes so he doesn't see them.

"Hey, look at me." I feel his hand along my shoulder.

I want to brush him off, but I don't have anymore fight left inside. I turn toward him, my eyes looking directly at his chest. He must not

like that, as the next moment, he holds my chin within his hands.
Lifting it clear up, so my eyes are aligned with his.

"You're safe with me." Bringing his forehead against mine, he looks deep
into my eyes.

"Come on, you can wear something of mine." He gives my lips
a quick kiss, grabs my hand and pulls me along behind him. The
further we walk into his dorm room, the more I realize how much
more extravagant this wing really is.

"I know you have a lot of questions." He turns his head slightly to the side
to look at me.

I simply nod my head, as we make it to a tall door at the end of the
hall. When he opens it, he allows me to walk in first. It's dark in here,
so when he flips the lights on it takes a moment for my eyes to adjust.

Once they do I look around, and my eyes are so large they must be out of
my head. This room alone can fit three of mine combined. It has a large king
size bed against the one wall, a large dresser diagonal from it. Looking across
from me, I see you step down a step, into another little room. That room looks
to be a makeshift office.

Shelves of books encompass every wall, with a giant mahogany desk in the
center. Three large windows, with a window seat are behind it. I find myself
walking toward it, without my knowledge. I don't get far, before his hand takes
a hold of my elbow. Looking back at him, I almost want to cry.

"I'll show you around soon. Right now, let's both get cleaned up and
dressed. Then, we can talk. Yeah?" He nods his chin at me as he asks the
question.

"That's probably a good idea." I say in a low tone, looking down at
myself.
"Follow me." He walks further into the room, opening another door.

This one opens to an extravagant bathroom. There's a double sink along one wall, a deep tub with jets on the far side, a little door I think has to lead to the toilet as it's nowhere in sight. I had been looking around, I didn't even realize the shower in the middle of the room. Until I hear the water being turned on. Looking at it, I see there are three shower heads, all of them spouting hot water.

He turns around to face me, mischief held deep in his eyes. Prowling to me, I can see he's up to something. I want to take a step back, but my body won't allow me to move. I'm frozen right here. Once he's in front of me, he doesn't say a word. Simply lifts my shirt clear from my body, throwing it behind him. His hand makes its way behind me to unclasp my bra with expertise.

When it falls down my arms, he shocks me when his eyes don't look down. They stay glaring right into mine.

"I'm going to get you clean now." His husky voice has wetness growing between my legs.

I don't fight him when he takes my hand, walking backwards, leading us to the shower. I'm so enamored, it completely escapes me that he said he was going to clean me. *Does that mean he's joining me?*

Chapter 24

Ezekiel

    It's taking all my willpower not to look at her glorious naked body. I can see everything she's thinking. Her feelings are written all over her face. My eyes don't move from hers, as I walk the both of us back towards my shower. The steam in the room, is making sweat build on her face. I can see a drip right on her lips, making it difficult for me to behave.

I take a step up, leading her right behind me. Once I feel the hot water hit my back in waves, I close my eyes, enjoying the sensation. Allowing the heat from the water to calm my raging beast.

"I have never seen a shower this big before." Her tone of wonderment has my eyes popping back open.

She looks like an angel, with her wide eyes, her head looking between each faucet that is pouring down on us. I release her hands, folding my arms over top my chest I watch my new fascination with an eagle eye. She refuses to look at me, disregarding my naked body all together. Her eyes make their way everywhere in the little space but at me.

Causing my head to fall back in laughter. The sound earning me her attention. She sticks her hip out, resting her hand there, the water cascading down her hair. I stand back, watching each droplet as it falls down the skin of her body. I have to swallow my need, turning around, I place my forehead along the cool tile.

I know she's not meaning to look sexy right now, but if I look at her a second longer like that, I'll take her here and now. It may even be without her permission, something I never do.

"You okay over there?" I hear her soft voice, knowing she wants to touch me, but she's holding herself back. I'm grateful for that.

Clearing my throat, I reach for the soap, lathering up my washcloth I keep in here.

"There should be some body wash over on the other side for you." My tone sounds short, but I can't help that.

I listen closely, as she turns away from me, opening the bottle, I hear the distinct sound of her squirting the substance on her hand.

The room fills with the scent of lavender, instantly calming me once more.

"It's not my body wash, or any other female visitor from me. It's Romans sisters. She comes to visit him and likes to stay the night sometimes." I feel I need to make it clear that I do not allow women to use this place.

I never bring the opposite sex to my room. Until now that is.

"Okay, I wasn't going to ask." I turn around to face her once more now that I'm calmer.

She is standing at my side, lathering up her smoking hot body. I watch her miniscule movements, allowing the water to wash away the bubbles on my body.

"So, what questions do you have?" Immediately, I change my tune.

Trying to be serious and determined to answer everything about our world. She turns to face me completely, eyes wide, biting that damn bottom lip of hers.

"You want to have this discussion here?" She holds out her hands, waving to the small room of the shower we stand in. I nod my head at her.

"Why not?" My brows furrow in confusion. She looks down at her naked body, then her eyes slowly prowl down mine.

I forget she grew up amongst humans. They are more shy when it comes to their bodies. In the werewolf world, this is a daily occurrence. It becomes your normal growing up since you're a young kid, and watching others form into wolves and back. Nakedness isn't anything unusual or shocking. Of course, with her all my normal rules go out the window.

Being this close to her, in this state, I find it absolutely difficult, but I know what she is ready for. As well as what she isn't, so we need to get used to this. Whether she likes it or not she will be staying with me from here on out. There will be many times we are both naked, and until she is ready for my cock, I have to become acquainted with not attacking her. Just because my wolf wants her.

She shrugs her shoulders once she sees I'm not budging.

"Okay, lets start with why you think I may be like you?" Her eyes make their way to mine, and I see sadness within hers.

"I went home for a few days. The time I had you pinned against the locker I saw your eyes change color." I hear the shocking intake of her breath.

Her mouth has fallen open, as her fingers go to touch her face.

"I take it you had no idea they did that?" She shakes her head at me, looking down at our feet.

"That only happens if you're a werewolf. Well, if you have any amount of Were blood in your family." She doesn't look up at me, it pisses me off. That is until I catch a scent of salt.

"Annabeth, hey look at me beautiful." I bring my hand below her chin, leading her eyes back to mine.

When I see the lone tear falling down her cheek, it guts me. Deciding she needs my arms wrapped around her for this talk, I turn the shower head off, and wrap her in my arms. Guiding her out of the door, I wrap her in a towel.

Still, she hasn't moved or talked, without hesitation I lift her into my arms and carry her to my bed.

"We are going to get your blankets wet." She squeaks out as I lay her down along the mattress.

Shrugging my shoulders, I scoot her over, as I lay beside her. With one arm, I gather her close to my side and run my fingers through her hair.

"Ask away baby. I'll tell you everything I know." I keep my voice quiet, so she knows I'm here for her through it all.

Annabeth

The feel of his hard body so close to mine is doing crazy things to my head. I both want to cuddle closer to him and push him away. I feel the need to scream and holler at him. That he's a liar and doesn't know what he is saying. When I look up through my hair, and see the truth held deep in his eyes, I find I can't utter a word.

"Is my mom," I pause for a moment.

Looking down at my hand along his well-defined chest. I play with the little bit of black hair there as I try to work through my thoughts. *Is my mother what? Is she a werewolf? Is she human? Do I get the blood from my father? Is she even my real mother?* That last thought scares me to my core.

Everyone has always said we look nothing alike. Causing my mother to cackle like a banshee, waving her hand in the air, brushing whoever said it off. Saying that I simply looked exactly like my father. I never questioned it since I had never known the man. The feel of his hand landing on top of mine, brings me out of my thoughts. My heart is stuttering, I bring my eyes up to look at him once more.

"She's not your mother at all." His words cause my heart to break.

It feels as though someone has taken a dagger to my most prized organ and stabbed me repeatedly with it. I get the distinct feeling of punching him over and over until this feeling goes away. If it ever does. I find my body can't stay still a moment longer. Without thinking about it, I stand from the bed, taking the towel with me and tying a knot over my chest so it stays.

Without a word said, I pace the end of his bed. I can feel my hands tear at my hair whenever I stop my movements. With my eyes closed, my body shaking, I feel like I may explode.

When I open my eyes, I look at the God like man, laying on his bed, completely naked, watching me like the wolf he is, expecting to eat his next meal.

"Who are my parents then?" With those words I know my life is about to change.

The second he tells me everything he knows; nothing will ever be the same again.

Chapter 25

Annabeth
I stand here in his room, with nothing but a towel covering my body. He's holding out his hand to me, beckoning me with his fingers to come to him. Honestly, I want nothing more than to be held in his arms, allowing him to make everything go away. Even if it's only for a little while.

Knowing what I want, not understanding why, I look to his bedroom door. I lift my foot, to take a step in that direction. Planning on leaving entirely, walking shamefully in nothing but this towel, smelling of him, back to my room.

"You could try," My eyes move back to him as he speaks up from where he still lays on the bed.

When I look at him, it's surprising how nonchalant he is right now. As though he doesn't have a care in the world. He's laying down, completely naked, with only his towel covering his most intimate part. Legs spread out, his arms are now behind his head. A look of mischief held in his eyes.

Licking my lips, as my entire mouth now feels dry, "Try what?" I go for innocence.

Pretending I don't understand what he's suggesting. A carnal smile forms on those beautiful red lips of his.

"To leave this room." He shrugs his shoulders at me.

"However, you and I both know I'll be able to catch you well before you make it."

His eyes are daring me to go for it. Taking a closer look, I can see he's practically begging me to do it.

"What will happen when you catch me?" My voice comes out breathy.

My thighs tightening with the knowledge that I don't want to admit to. With a wave of his hand, he tells me, "Why don't you try it and find out for yourself?"

There's an edge to his voice. One of his brows raises with a challenge. I know he wants that more than anything right now. The real question is *do I?*

Ezekiel

I am begging her to make one small move towards that door. My wolf is dying for a chase. I see she's at war with herself once more. Her eyes go from me to the door, and back again. Her eyes fall to her hands, that have such a tight grip on the towel, her knuckles are turning white. As though she doesn't trust herself if the material falls at her feet.

One thing is for certain, she cannot trust me if that happens. I've been hanging on by a thread this entire time. It's bound to snap soon.

"Who are my real parents, and how did the woman I thought is my mother find me?" Slowly, her eyes make their way back up to mine.

I look away from her, up toward the ceiling. Thinking of how I want to answer that question.

"Come to the bed, and I'll tell you everything I know." My voice comes out low and in a partial growl.

My wolf wants nothing more than for her to be near us. The closer her body is to me the more control I'll have over that piece of thread. She tiptoes back to the bed, sitting down on the opposite side. Leaving a bit of space between our bodies.

I allow that for now, as I turn my body to face her. Propped on my elbow, I hold my head in the palm of my hand as I explain what I was able to find out.

"Your real family are known as the Delaney's. They are a very powerful Werewolf race, and your father was the most powerful." Her eyes widen at the information.

"Your mother came from the long line of Hadley's, the most powerful witches known in our world. When she fell in love with your father, she was cast out of the family, as they never mix with any other beings."

At that information she looks sad. Biting her lip, she looks down at our now joined hands. It's the only thing that I can think of doing, to bring her some kind of comfort.

"She was cast out for falling in love with a werewolf?" Her tear-filled eyes find mine.

I nod my head as I continue on with the story of the past she never knew about.

"Your father and mine were best friends at the time, but they found disagreements with their views on our world. Causing tension between our families." I scoot closer to her, feeling my towel falling from the movement.

"They realized what we were to one another, and I'm not certain what was the deciding factor, but they chose to run with you. So, we would never meet." Her mouth falls open. I can see the burning questions clearly through her eyes staring back at me.

"Why though? I don't understand why they would do that."

"The only conclusion I can come up with is that they wanted nothing to do with my family, or our world after things became too conflicting." I shrug my shoulders.

"Of course, they knew that if we grew up together, I would never have let you go." She looks up at me once more, biting that sensational lip of hers.

"You wouldn't have?" Her question makes me laugh.

It's a dark noise, one that shows a bit more of my rueful side than I care to.

"Oh, little lamb, there's no way I'm allowing you to ever leave me again." A carnal smile forms on my lips as I watch her body squirm. I can see the battle going on inside of her.

It mirrors back at me within her eyes. There's a big part of her that is already mine, but a smaller part. The one that grew up in the human world wants to tell me where to go and how to get there. Little does she know I grew up in Hell.

My body is wrought with tension, as I already know what her next move is going to be. Quickly she stands from the bed, ringing her fingers together.

"You cannot say things like that to me and expect me to be okay with it."

Leaning back along my pillow, knowing full well my cock is growing hard, I act as though I have no care in the matter. Shrugging my shoulders, I tell her so.

"You may not like my approach, but the fact of the matter is you are mine, and I am yours. Nothing will change that."

Looking deep into her eyes I tell her truthfully, "As far as I'm concerned no one in this world, human, witch, or werewolf alike will take you from me."

With those words her eyes grow cold. She glares at me one final time before she begins walking to my bedroom door. I count to five in my head, giving her a head start. After all the chase is half the fun.

Chapter 26

A <u>nnabeth</u>

I can't believe the audacity of this man! Exclaiming that I am his and have no say in the matter. I got news for him; I didn't grow up in this world of his. I have a mind of my own, opinions that matter. I will not allow any man to tell me how to feel or what to think. Right now, I feel he is being disrespectful beyond what is acceptable.

I stand from the bed, telling him what I think before I turn away from him, giving him my back and walking away. I know this is all a game to him in some way, but to me this is my life. Until he can acknowledge that, I will not be giving him any sort of attention. I make it to the door, thinking perhaps he's going to be reasonable, and let me leave his dormitory so I can calm down.

I take one step out from his room, then that thought leaves my mind all together. As a long muscular arm is wrapped around my center, lifting me up clear off the ground. I'm now halfway in the air, my feet kicking away, as I try to punch the arm that is around my body to no avail.

If anything, my antics only make him laugh sardonically in my ear, as he pulls my back to his chest. The excursion of his actions knocking the breath from my lungs. Still, I carry on fighting, not giving up in the slightest. My body squirming, moving along his, with me trying to break free is making him harder. I feel his manhood standing at attention, touching my ass cheeks. If he moves just an inch, he could be cocooned between them if he really wanted. That thought shouldn't turn me on as much as it does.

It isn't until we hear a hoarse laugh coming from the living area, that we realize we are no longer alone. Both sets of our eyes rise up, to see his roommate and best friend standing there by a bookshelf. He's bent over, hand on his stomach, practically crying with the excursion of his laughter.

I expect Ezekiel to place me down onto my feet. Instead, he simply maneuvers us, so his back is to his friend, and his front along with myself are away from the prying eyes. *Well now what? Is he finally going to let me leave?*

Ezekiel

I had no idea Roman had returned to our dorm. I was so preoccupied with my little lamb; I must have missed the signs all together.

"When did you get back?" I ask in a harsh tone.

I watch as my best friend stands at his full height, the tone of my voice alerting him I'm not to be played with. All humor has left his face.

Clearing his throat, he answers me with wide eyes, "Well, I couldn't find any entertainment." He simply shrugs his shoulders, not removing his eyes from mine.

I feel confused for a moment, until he nods his head to the mirror above our fireplace. With confusion overriding all thought, I place Annabeth on her feet, instructing her to get back in my room. She turns around, hands on her hips ready to tell me off. One look at my face has her taking a step back, mouth agape.

With a lift of my eyebrow, and a nod of my head I instruct her to do as I say. She turns away from me, faster than I like, and walks to my ensuite bathroom. Slamming the door behind her. The little act of defiance of hers is going to get her ass spanked.

Lifting my head up toward my ceiling, I pray to the Gods for patients. Something tells me I'm going to need a lot of it with her. I hear a low laugh coming from my right, causing my eyes to fall once more to my best friend. A look of disdain written all over my face.

"Man, you have to look in the mirror. I'm telling you it's important." He walks closer to the fireplace, standing in front waiting for me to join him.

With a roll of my eyes in annoyance, I walk over to where he stands, looking at my reflection. I, myself, take a step back at what I see.

This has never happened to me before. I am flaring, with golden eyes, as yellow as the sun. Stepping closer I bring my hand to my face, just to make sure I'm seeing correctly.

"It has to be because of her. That's the only explanation." Roman whispers.

"I don't understand. This only happens when we get emotional. I am one who is never emotional around anyone. You know that." I dumbly say.

Causing my best friend to smirk at me. His reflection showing the side of his mouth lifting up, mischief held in his eyes.

"Seems that has changed immensely."

He moves closer to my body, placing his hand along my shoulder.

"Welcome to the world of emotions. They are a bitch to have, but you get used to them after a while." He shrugs his shoulders, with a laugh.

Dropping his hand, he walks towards the kitchen. "I take it you told her everything?"

Looking away from the mirror, I crack my neck, trying to get the tension to release from my body.

"Yeah, everything I know anyway." I take a seat at the counter, watching as he rummages through the cupboard. He's knocking things over, making a bunch of noise until he finally finds what he was looking for.

As he turns around, he has two shot glasses held in his hand.

"I think you need this right now." He places them on the countertop, turning to retrieve the tequila we have hidden, and when he comes back, he pours us both some. We are quiet as we take a few, the burning sensation making its way down my throat, settling in my stomach the feeling divine.

"So, now what?" He asks slamming down his shot glass, his blood shot eyes looking at me.

"Now I have you get the car started and wait for us out front of the building. I think it's time we paid my father and her mother a little visit."

Without another word, he walks to the door, grabbing the keys. I close my eyes, allowing the alcohol in my system, to calm me once more. Before, I have to go into my room, and get my aggravating mate.

Chapter 27

Annabeth

I find myself sitting on his bed, contemplating everything I have recently learned. It's hard to believe that my whole entire life has been nothing but a lie. The more I think about it, the more I want to scream. I would love to say it isn't true, that everything he is saying is fabricated. However, seeing him turn into a wolf right in front of my eyes, and the fact that I can see the truth staring back at me as he tells me what he found out makes that extremely difficult to do.

The sound of the door opening has me lifting my head. I don't understand it, but the sight of Ezekiel has my eyes welling up with tears. As he slowly walks closer to me, I want to do nothing more than look down at the floor. Anywhere, but at him. However, for a reason I'm not sure of I keep my eyes focused on the man I barely know, but feel the strongest connection with out of everyone in my life.

Once he's standing in front of me, his hand reaches out to take hold of my chin. Lifting my head, so he can see my eyes more clearly, I feel the first of the tears fall down the skin of my cheek. I watch him closely as he wipes the remnants away with his thumb. Causing more to fall in their place.

He looks at the little droplets with a fascination held deep in his eyes. With the look of dismay and wonder all over his face, I find myself questioning if he has ever really cared about someone crying before. I half expect him to drop his hand from my face, wipe away the wetness that is now along his fingers, and dismiss me all together. Walking to the door giving me some sort of demand.

In reality, he surprises me entirely. He moves his body closer to mine, knocking my knees with his. With his free hand, he spreads my legs open wide enough for him to fit between. He kneels in front of me, right in between, rubbing his hardness against my awakening center.

I give a low moan, and the bastard smiles. Knowing exactly what he's doing to me. With both his hands, he takes a hold of my ass, sliding me even closer to his body. We are so close now our noses are touching. Every breath he takes, I feel along my lips. Opening my mouth, my tongue practically falls out of my mouth.

"Soon little lamb," Bringing his lips closer to mine, he moves them just above my own. It is taking everything I have not to move the centimeter closer, having the kiss I crave.

"Right now, we need to leave." He rubs his hands along my thighs. Feathering down my skin, then back up just the same.

Distracting me, my eyes move to my legs. Watching his movements, secretly hoping he brings his hands to my center where I need him the most. His words finally make sense a moment later, and my head pops up to look him in the eyes.

"Where are we going?" I'm a little frightened to hear his answer. Although I'm certain in my mind where we will be going.

Ezekiel

She asks, but I can see deep in her eyes she already knows the answer to her own question. I know she's scared to see the woman that she has always known to be her mother. Looking at her in person may bring everything to a head, but I strongly believe that needs to happen. Lifting my hand, I take her chin once more, rubbing my thumb along the skin of her cheek.

I have never felt this way with anyone else in my life. I feel like I constantly have to be touching her. If I'm not, I feel the stirrings of my wolf about ready to come out. Bending my head down, I bring our foreheads together. Closing my eyes, I take this moment we have together to breath her in. Allowing her scent to calm both me and the beast within.

Once I open my eyes again, I get a sudden feeling of determination deep in the pit of my stomach.

"I will be with you the entire time. Through all that is to come." Her eyes move between mine, gauging for the truth she can clearly see held in mine.

"Promise?" That one word breaks my soul. The sound of her voice broken; the fear held within.

Cupping her face, I lightly kiss her lips. "You have my word; I will be with you from here on out."

A light smile falls upon her lips. She's happy about this now, but I wonder how she will feel when she finds out just how serious I am about this. There is no way she's being away from me.

A werewolf needs to be with his soul mate, his other half once they find one another. Otherwise, both can go mad and crazy. There would be no telling what I could do if she isn't by my side. Meaning she will have to move into the dormitory with me, have all my classes, and for the first few months I need to be touching her as much as possible.

Especially, since we aren't mating. I won't do that until I know she's ready for that step. So to make my wolf calm, making sure we both don't go insane, I will need to have her skin beneath mine in some way at all times. I will make sure my father tells the school what's going on, and knowing how much of an asshole I already am I'm certain there will be no objections.

Not unless they want me to be a million times worse. Not to mention, if I cannot control the wolf part of me, I will be changing almost nonstop. Running around the estate of the school just to find her. If *he* gets any kind of power over my human side, while she's away from us there is no telling what he would do. There's a possibility my wolf could even hurt her in his fever to have her with us. I won't allow that to happen.

So, even if the dean, professors, and students don't like it. Tough shit! I know she will fight me on this whole situation. She was raised in the human world and does not understand how bad things can get for me. Eventually, she would understand because the longer she's in our world the more her wolf will awaken.

She will feel the exact same persistence I feel. The fever of need coursing through my veins will hit her tenfold. Women werewolves, being away from their mates for a long amount of time, especially in the beginning, have it so much worse. It's as though their bodies go into a pseudo-heat. Causing them to feel like their bodies are on fire, and in constant pain. I won't allow that to happen to my little lamb.

"We need to have a conversation with my father, and to see if your mother and Arthur are back from their trip yet." Her eyes furrowed in confusion at that information.

Apparently, the lying little bitch didn't even tell her that they were leaving to visit Arthur's relatives. They live on another werewolf estate, about an hour away from ours.

They wanted a space all their own. Arthur chose to live under my father's rule because he understands how to help him more with his sadistic needs. His own father was about to give up on him, kick him out of our pack entirely, but my father hadn't wanted that. Knowing how crazy Arthur is, and what he would likely do if that happened.

"Come on, I'll explain on the way there I promise." I stand up, reaching my hand out to her to help her up from our bed.

Once she's standing in front of me, I don't understand why, but I wrap my arms around her. Cocooning her in a warm hug. I just feel like this is what she needs before we leave. Especially, since I know her life is about to change immensely after we have this discussion.

Chapter 28

Annabeth

I sit in the passenger seat of his ride, my body numb. I haven't spoken a word since we left. I'm too afraid I'll say the wrong thing, ask the wrong questions, or just sound completely stupid with my words. After all, my thoughts are barely making any sense to me at the moment. If I were to speak, I highly doubt he would understand anything.

Looking out the window, at the trees as they go by, calms my racing emotions. We have about an hour and a half drive to get back to his father's estate. I guess it's really the pack's home, but I have enough to worry about to be thinking about that information. I place my arm along the door, holding my head in my hand. Closing my eyes I think of all the things I've recently learned.

Somehow, my mother isn't really who she says she is. Meaning one way or another she has lied to me. Either not telling me the truth about her origin, and what she possesses in her bloodline, or she isn't my mother at all. That thought breaks my heart. It would mean all this time I have lived with a stranger. Whereas, I thought she only recently became a stranger these last few months.

I'm doing what I can to fight back the tears that want to fall from my eyes. I don't want Zeek to see me this way. The burn at the tip of my nose lets me know that I am about to fail miserably in my endeavor if I don't think about something else.

My eyes pop open at the inferno I feel as his big hand engulfs mine. I find myself looking at our joined fingers. Watching as his thumb rubs along the skin of my hand.

"It's going to be okay. We will figure this out together." He says in a low voice.

Lifting my eyes, I look at the man that is behind the wheel. He looks like a God with his muscular, tattooed arms stretched out in front of him. He must feel my stare as his eyes leave the road and cut to me. I can see his nostrils move as he takes a deep breath.

Slowly, he turns, bringing his attention back on the road, as he moves about on his seat. Releasing my hand, I watch in fascination, as he lifts it between his legs. Shifting the obvious tenting happening there, he growls with annoyance.

"You really need to change the direction of your thoughts." He grumbles, bringing his now golden eyes to face me.

"Otherwise, I will pull off to the side, and take you here and now in this truck."

He watches as my tongue shoots out, licking my lips. Causing them to moisten, as I swallow down the moan that wants to work up my throat. His eyes move to watch it move as I do this.

Closing his eyes for a brief second, he licks his own lips, as his hand falls to my thigh. Ever so lightly he feathers his fingers along the skin of my leg. Up and back down, just to do the motion over and over again.

"If we weren't so close, I would stop this truck, and put both of us out of our misery."

I'm not certain if he means he would do me here in the back seat of his truck, or just help me have an orgasm another way. Whichever, I find myself biting my bottom lip, as my eyes move to the back seat of his vehicle.

The sound of his predatory laughter has my eyes shooting back to him.

"Do not tempt me little lamb. I'm hanging on by a thread here." His voice sounds gravely.

When he looks back at me, his eyes are still golden, but I feel something else looking at me entirely. It takes me a moment before I realize his wolf is at the forefront. Looking directly at me. The sight of his eyes has my heart racing.

"Fuck it." That voice, I know, must belong to the wolf within.

It sounds nothing like Ezekiel. He pulls the truck over, deep into a path along the trees, bringing us to a sudden stop. He pulls the emergency break, as his hand reaches for my buckle. He unclips it and drags me across the center to his lap before I can even blink.

The next moment his lips are on mine, with his tongue deep in my mouth, dueling with my own. The taste of this man drives me crazy. I bring both my hands to his hair, pulling the strands as I rub my center along his hardness. Bringing the feel of euphoria through my body. His lips fall from mine, as he kisses down my neck, to my collar bone.

A moan escapes my mouth, as I pull him even closer to me. Both his hands land on my hips, as he moves them along his hardness in a rough way, causing a sensation to grow deep below. I'm not certain, but I think I may orgasm from this action alone.

"Not yet." He whispers along my skin. As he lifts us up, laying me down, my back along the long front seat.

"I want to feel your spasm on my tongue." His words bring me to the edge.

I cannot believe how filthy this man can be, or how much I love it. He strips my jeans down my legs, and since he ripped my underwear earlier, he doesn't take long for his face to dive between my legs.

I'm panting like a cat in heat. I feel his lips along my thighs, kissing me up, across just above where I need him the most, going down my other thigh.

"Oh, come on." I whine, causing him to laugh. The feel of his breath tickles my sex.

"Patience baby. The thrill of what's to come is part of the fun."

Ezekiel

I know it's important we get to the estate so we can find out all the information she needs, but the scent of her arousal filling my truck is too much for me to take. I just need to calm my beast down for a moment so I can focus on the rest of the drive there. Otherwise, I could very well cause a car accident.

I tease her for a few minutes, enjoying the sight of her womanhood leaking just for me. My mouth waters, as I look at her essence slide down her pussy lips, to the crack of her ass, and onto the seat below. I'm never washing my truck again. I want that scent to fill my nostrils every time I'm going somewhere.

Not being able to hold back a second longer, I take my fingers and open her lips. Looking up at her, I see she has her eyes closed, her hands having a death grip on my head. With my tongue flat, I give her one long lick. From the tip of her ass, all the way up to her little nub.

"Fuck yes." She whisper yells. Causing me to laugh once more.

I love when my little lamb curses, it turns me on all the more. My wolf is raging in my head. Pacing back and forth, wanting to devour our mate here and now, but I know she's a virgin. With the mood I'm in I'll hurt her with my need to take her roughly. I won't allow that to happen.

Instead, I bury my face into her pussy and devour her that way. Her hips lift up, begging me for more. I oblige, by brining my thumb to her clit and rubbing in slow circles as I eat the most delicious meal I've ever had. I hear her whimpering but can't understand the words she is trying to say.

The only coherent words falling from my little lamb's mouth that are comprehensible are 'please' and 'more.' With my free hand, I unzip my pants, diving in to grab a hold of my cock. With every dip of my tongue into her wetness, I pump my hand up and down my shaft. Knowing she's close, I speed up my antics, trying to finish at the same time as her.

I feel the sudden pressure building in my balls, letting me know how close I am. I dive my tongue deep into her body, as I speed up the circular motion of my thumb along her clit. The next second, she's gushing on my tongue, as I feel my release along my hand. I keep my tongue inside enjoying the feel of her muscles spasming, grabbing my appendage and squeezing it profusely. It makes me want to rip these pants off and thrust myself deep inside.

Her screams ring in my ears, as they echo through the windows. She's so loud I have to look up once she settles down. Making sure the glass didn't break in the process. Once I see every window is fine, I spread kisses just below her belly button, before laying my head down on her stomach. Looking up at her, with the look of pure euphoria on her face, brings calmness to my wolf once more. I get the sudden thought of her with a ring on her hand, and a growing belly.

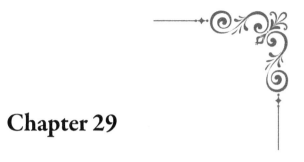

Chapter 29

A nnabeth

Coming down from the euphoria of my orgasm, I'm suddenly feeling very relaxed. Looking down I see Ezekiel looking at me with a strange and thoughtful look on his face.

"What is that look for?" My voice comes out breathy.

He only smiles, as he sorts out my clothes once more. Lifting me up in my seat, he kisses my lips, before straightening my body, so I'm sitting forward once more.

"Buckle up." He whispers, the sound of his voice making me squirm in the seat.

I do as I'm told, basically being on autopilot at the moment. Without a word, he puts the truck into drive, and we spend the remaining ride in silence. The scent of sex fills the truck. The sound of him licking his fingers has me turning my face to the side.

I see him watching me, instead of the road. Normally, I would chastise him about that, but as he slowly places the three fingers he had inside of me earlier, now in his mouth, to suck the remnants of what we just did. I quickly face the front, looking out the windshield, as I feel my cheeks redden with embarrassment.

The sound of his laughter has me licking my canines in aggravation. I don't know how or when, but I do know I'll make him pay for that.

"I look forward to it." He lifts my hand with him, bringing it to his mouth and he kisses my fingers.

Focusing on the road once more, I see we are at the front gate of the estate. All the happy endorphins, coursing through my body, are gone. In their place, stone cold fear.

"Relax, I'm right here with you." He whispers sweet words before placing my hand along the middle seat and opening his window.

He talks to the guards for a moment, each set of eyes looking at me while they converse. Seeing their nasals move with the deep breaths they take in, lets me know they can smell what just took place only moments earlier. I slide down the seat, trying to hide within the hoodie he let me borrow. What they must all think of me.

"They won't think a damn thing, or else they know I'll take care of them." The sound of determination in Ezekiel's voice has me turning my head his way.

He stares me down, his eyes a golden color. "How do you always know what I'm thinking?" My words come out so low, I'm shocked even with his werewolf hearing that he heard what I said.

"It's a mate thing." He grumbles below his breath, as he drives through the gate, and down the long driveway.

The closer we come to the mansion at the end, the faster my heart beats. He reaches for my hand once more, engulfing my small one with his larger. The heat of his skin brings a calming feeling to my body.

"I haven't really met your father and mother. I'm not sure what they will think of me or have to say about my history." I swallow down the acid that is building within the bottom of my throat.

I think I may be sick. He drives around the large fountain, that is placed right in front of the mansion. He places his truck in park and unsnaps his belt buckle. He undoes mine next and pulls me to his mouth faster than I can think.

He's doing what he knows will help me forget. Taking away all the fear I'm feeling in the moment and replacing it with a distraction I've quickly grown to crave. The tip of his tongue licks my lips, asking for them to open. When I do, he plunges inside, fighting aggressively with mine. Swallowing every moan that falls from my lips.

When he pulls back, his hands are on both sides of my head. "I will be with you every step of the way. You don't have to worry about that."

He reaches for my hand, bringing it to his heart, and holds it there. His own hand placed on top of mine.

The feel of his steady heartbeat brings me comfort. "You have me forever little lamb."

I laugh at the nickname he gave me only weeks ago. "Well, according to you I'm not just human, so I think that name doesn't fit anymore," I tell him with a tilt of my head and a raised brow.

He brings his face so close to mine, I find myself holding my breath, waiting to see what he does next.

"You'll always be my lamb baby, and I'll be the big bad wolf that will enjoy eating you alive." He kisses my chin before nipping it.

The sound of footsteps moving closer to his driver's side door has me looking away from him.

The sight of the same older gentleman, in the butler uniform, comes to a halt just in front of the truck. He reaches out, opening the door for us, as he nods his head at Ezekiel.

"Young gentleman. Good to see you today." He gives off a solemn laugh, causing Zeek to smile at him.

It's the first time I've seen him look at someone with dare I say a hint
of love held in his eyes. Besides me of course.

"Hello there Joseph. I believe you have heard of Annabeth here?" He waves
his hand in front of me, causing the older gentleman's eyes to make their way to
me.

I jump almost falling from the truck at the man's eyes. They are pure
white, meaning....

I look at Zeek, and he has a sad smile on his lips as he studies me closely.

"Up with you now little lamb, we need to get this shit over with." He
grumbles a moment later.

Joseph catches my hand with his and escorts me from the vehicle.
"Yes, I've heard wonderful things about Annabeth here." He smiles
at me, a tight grip on my hand.

"Now, now Joseph. You wouldn't be putting the moves on my mate now,
would you?" He asks the older gentleman with a tilt of his head.

Causing a boisterous laugh to fall from the older man's lips. "I
wouldn't dream of it, sir." He places my hand in Zeek's, bowing his
head, as he walks off.

I watch the older man, feeling perplexed by how well he knows the land.
Not once has he bumped into something or fallen.

"He saved me when I was a pup." Those words have my mouth agape,
as my eyes shoot to him once more.

"What happened?" He rubs his thumb over the back of my hand,
looking into my eyes, with such sadness. He almost looks like a small
boy once more.

The clearing of the throat has us looking toward the front of the mansion. There stands a tall man, built just the same as Ezekiel. With his shoulders straight, I can see from this distance, that both men share the same chin and nose. As he walks us closer to the man in the shadows, it becomes clear just who he is.

Once we are in front of him, Zeek, now looking like the fierce young man I met that first night, stares the older man down. There's not much height difference between the two. His father was only an inch or two taller. When his eyes make their way to me, I can see he too has blue eyes. However, they are nowhere near as beautiful as Zeek's. Leaving me wondering if he got his eyes from his mother.

"Hello, Miss Delaney." The stern man's face doesn't change at all.

My brows furrow with confusion. "Who is Miss Delaney? My name is Annabeth Corbett." That makes a predatory smile form along his lips.

Chapter 30

A͟n͟n͟a͟b͟e͟t͟h͟
I find myself looking at the back of the man that has yet to answer me. All he did was give me a smile, and then turned to walk further into the mansion. Ezekiel and I close behind him.

"Are you ever going to answer my question?" My tone comes out confrontational. I can feel the tension growing in Ezekiel's body.

I'm guessing he half expects his father to turn around and holler at me or tell me to watch my tone. Surprisingly, he only turns around to face me once he's at a large chair off to the side in the living room. He glares at me, an eyebrow raised, as he tilts his head to the side.

"Which question is that, Miss Delaney?" His tone is petulant.

Grinding my teeth, I feel I need to place my hands in my sweater pockets. Otherwise, I may do something suicidal.

"Why do you keep calling me Miss Delaney? My name for the fourth time is Annabeth Corbett." I can feel my body vibrating with anger.

Not only is this large man, calling me by a name I do not know, but he's standing there looking as though he's studying me. Refusing to give me a proper answer.

"I think we need to wait for your mother to arrive before we get into this conversation." He says his voice sounding strained with tension, as he sits down in the large chair.

His back straight, his arms laying upon the chair, his fingers spread out, holding onto the end of the leather. The sound of him clearing his throat has my heart practically jumping from my chest into mine.

Within seconds, an older woman walks into the room, by a door I hadn't seen. It blends well with the side paneling of the wall.

"I have your bourbon, my lord." She bows her head, the name she is calling him making my eyebrows shoot up.

So high they may very well be a part of my hair now. Without taking his eyes away from me, he reaches for the small glass, bringing the drink to his mouth. I watch as his throat moves with the movement of him swallowing the golden liquid.

"Why don't the both of you have a seat." At his words, I see Ezekiel move to one of the small couches in the room.

Before he takes a seat, he walks over to me and takes hold of my hand.

"Come on." His words whispered in my ear.

I allow him to lead me, too nervous to remove my eyes from looking at his father.

When we sit down, only then does a carnal smile form on his lips. I watch as he so easily lifts a hand, dismissing the older woman from the room. Without a word, or any other movement she turns and walks out the side door once again. My brows furrow in confusion as I look around the large room.

"Where's your mother?" I bring my face towards Ezekiel, asking the question in a hushed tone.

Briefly, I turn my head to face the gorgeous man sitting beside me. Awaiting for him to answer, even though at the moment he looks down at our joined hands. I watch as his throat moves, with a look of sadness taking over his features.

"My wife is asleep right now. She does that throughout most of her day." The sound of his father's strong baritone causes me to jump in my seat.

Whipping my head to face him, I look between the two good looking men in the room with me. There's something about his mother, that neither are sharing. Judging by Ezekiel's face, that's not something he wants to tell me at the moment. Opening my mouth, I start to tell him it's okay, that we can discuss it at a later time, when the sound of footsteps entering the room, has my lips shutting.

Looking up, I see the woman I have only ever known as my mother. Standing up, I try to walk over to where she stands, beside that asshole she calls her husband, but Ezekiel holds my hand in a death grip. Not showing any signs of releasing me.

"What the hell happened to you?" My voice comes out broken.

The sight of the once strong woman, standing before me, with a black eye and bruises along both arms.

Seeing her in this condition causes blue flaming of anger to course through my veins.

"Somebody better answer me. Right now." I'm grinding my teeth so hard, I'm afraid they may break under the pressure.

"She and I have been enjoying one another in some different ways, in the bedroom." Arthur answers me, a slimy smile forming along his lips. My mother gives me a simple nervous smile in return.

"What the fuck did you do to her you monster!" I yell so loud, my voice echoes off the walls.

I begin fighting like a banshee, trying to break free from Ezekiel's hold. Which has only become more tightly, as he stands from the couch, wrapping his arms around my entire body.

"We cannot do anything; it's not how things work in our world." He whispers along the skin of my neck. His words only make me punch, slap, and hit him that much harder.

"You all knew he was doing this to her and allowed him to. What the fuck is wrong with all of you?" Turning my body, I hit his chest repeatedly.

Tears pouring down my cheeks, with gut wrenching screams falling from my lips.

"I know little lamb. I wish I could change things, but that takes time." He tightens his hold around me a little more. Causing the air to be sucked straight from my lungs.

Within his hold, there is no way I can continue to move, nor make any noise. The only sound filling the room are my pants, as my chest hits his muscular one with every deep breath I take. Finally, I succumb to my weakness, looking up into his eyes.

I know he means what he has said to me. The truth is there looking back at me. Along with a hint of sadness, his blue green eyes stare directly into mine.

"Breath with me. We need to calm your heart rate" My brows furrow in confusion, as I don't understand why he feels I need to calm down so much.

That is until slowly, he moves one of his arms from around my body, placing his hand along mine and he lifts it up at the side of our bodies. There has to be something wrong here, my eyes must be playing tricks on me. I move my eyes away from his, to look at our joined hands, to see if what I think is in my peripheral vision is really there.

My mouth falls open at the sight before me. My nails have grown longer, looking more like black claws rather than fingernails. It looks more like a paw, the smaller form covered in what looks to be grey and silver fur. Knowing I'm too stunned right now to do any harm to Arthur, he releases my body, so I can lift both hands in between our bodies.

He's still standing close to me just in case he needs to pull me to him again. Holding me still so I don't harm Arthur or worse hurt myself. These claws that are a part of my hand look sharp. On a sob, I look from the paws in front of me, to the young man that has filled every aspect of my life within these few days I have known him.

I can feel tears, sadness, and confusion welling in my eyes.

"What is happening to you right now is completely normal." At his words, my eyes fall back to where my hands used to be.

"What's happening to me?" My voice comes out hoarse, as the first of my tears fall from my eyes, rolling down my cheek.

Chapter 31

E zekiel
The sound of her whimpers and the sight of her tears breaks my heart. All I really want to do right now is celebrate. The wolf part of her is waking up now, meaning if we play our cards right she will go through her first change very soon. A carnal feeling runs through my veins at the thought. I know the best way to help her through this, and I will thoroughly enjoy it.

The feel of her body shuddering against my chest has those steamy thoughts vanishing. Shaking my head, I quickly remember where we are and what's happening around us right now.

"How could he?" She whispers into my chest.
Her hands are full of my shirt, as she squeezes the material in her fists.

I don't even have to ask who she is talking about. I know all too well, that my father is a miserable, sadistic asshole. He's the reason I am who I have become over the years. He hasn't ever hit my mother or any woman. That is one thing he himself doesn't believe in, but it doesn't mean he stops any member of the pack from doing it.

"I'm fine sweetheart. Really." Her mother's voice cuts into the moment, her tone sounding defeated.

Causing Annabeth to raise her head from my chest, whip it around and glare at the pathetic excuse of a man standing beside her mother. I feel the tension growing within her body once more. Finding myself, tightening my arms around her center again.

Good thing I did, as she shoves at me, screaming like a banshee. "You son of a bitch! I'll fucking kill you. You're nothing but a piece of shit!"

She's swinging her arms all around, trying to break from my hold. Knowing I can't let her do that if she attacks him, it could be bad. She doesn't understand the dynamics of the pack life yet.

"Let go of me, I'm going to tear his heart from his chest." She pants, as her body is growing ferocious.

The sound of laughter ringing in my ear, makes me tighten my hold all the more. Once she hears the sound, she freezes, all of her movements coming to a complete stop. As her head turns toward the large man sitting on his throne. Watching as his play works out in front of him, his puppets doing as he says.
"Isn't this touching." My father looks down at his nails.

Sitting there as though everything is suddenly boring him. "You..."

Annabeth takes a step forward, quickly I drag her back to me. She hits my chest so hard, she bounces off me, with a thud. The breath leaves from her chest with the contact of my hard chest. Knowing she doesn't understand, but that she is in danger if she finishes that sentence, I hold her tightly.

My entire upper body wrapped around her. My mouth so close to her ear, I nip her earlobe, doing what I can to gain her attention.

"Don't little lamb." I'm praying from my pleading tone; she understands why I am saying those three little words.

I'm not on his side, I am completely, and fully on hers. This is why as I see her mouth open wide, her eyes glaring at my father, I cover her mouth with my hand.

"You don't understand baby girl," I call her the sweet endearment, trying to get her to listen.

Hoping that she will comprehend and stop talking. To my utter shock, she finally listens, her entire body relaxing against mine. She turns her face toward me, looking at me out of the corner of her eye. She places her hand above mine, gliding it down to her chin.

"Why shouldn't I?" Her voice comes out breathy.

I know she's not meaning to cause a distraction for me, but with the sight of her all worked up, breathing hard, and all her womanly curves against me. I have to adjust my lower half away from her delectable ass.

"You don't know what he's capable of," I whisper back. Emotion showing on my face.

She studies me for a few moments, before giving me a slight nod of her head. The message in her eyes is quite clear though. She's not letting this slide; we will be discussing this later. Turning back toward my father, who has a demonic smile along his lips. His fingers along his chin, tilting his head to the side, squinting his eyes, he studies her intently right back.

"I want that monster out of the room for this conversation." Her shoulders straighten, a look of determination filling her eyes.

My father grows excited at the challenge, sitting up from his chair, he places his elbows to his knees. Biting his bottom lip, he gives off a demonic laugh, before his eyes move away from my woman, and to the piece of shit standing behind us.

"Leave the room, Arthur." His tone is demanding.

The type that will cause a grown man to cry if he tries to argue. My eyes focus entirely on my father, as I watch his eyebrow raise. Knowing full well, from that one look alone, that he's waiting to see what the man behind us will do. It takes a few minutes, but slowly I hear Arthur's footsteps walking from the room.

I hear her mother sigh behind us, the tension in the room lessening. She relaxes against my chest, her breathing following mine, as I take a breath in and let it out. Knowing she's following my lead; I make sure to take a few more soothing breaths.

"Good girl." I drag my teeth against the skin of her neck. Announcing to her privately how much I will make her feel good later on tonight.

Judging by the goosebumps growing on the skin of her arms, she has received my message loud and clear. A devilish sound falls from my lips. A smile forms on my face, so close she can feel it along her skin.

"If you two are finished with the foreplay." My father's tone sounds annoyed.

Looking up from Annabeth's neck, I see him glaring at me. He hates how I can treat my woman this way. Be inclined by thinking of her, actually caring for this beauty standing in front of me.

I wink at him, causing a growl to make its way up his throat and out of his mouth. She stands stiff at the noise. Her reaction makes me smug. Now I know she only gets hot and bothered when the noise comes from my mouth.

"Come on baby girl. We can sit over on the couch." I grab her hand and walk in front of her. Guiding her, as I block her from the monster's sight. Protecting her the only way I can right now.

When I sit down, I pull her down beside me. Turning my body into her, I wrap my arm around her shoulders. My eyes don't move away from my very pissed-off father, as we hear the small footsteps coming from her mother. As she takes a seat in the chair across from us. Annabeth reaches for my other hand, which is placed on my thighs.

Causing my eyes to break away from my father and down at our joined fingers. I feel floured that someone actually is touching me for strength and comfort. She's the only person in this world to ever seek out my touch.

Not in a sexual way, but in an emotional and supportive way. Causing the air to break from my lungs. Making me feel as though I can't breathe. Looking up from our joined hands, I make my way up her arms, to her collar bone, I take a deep breath, preparing myself for what I may see when I finally make eye contact with her.

Raising my eyes, I slowly peruse her neck, to her chin. Landing on her lips. I keep my eyes focused on that mouth of hers for a moment. The pink, plump part of her body I suddenly want to attack with all the passion working its way into me.

Finally, I make it to her eyes and feel amazed at what I see staring back at me. If I wasn't sitting down, I would fall right to my knees. Wrapping my arms around her legs, begging her to look at me this way forever.

A clearing of a throat breaks our connection a second later, as she glares over my shoulder. My shoulders fall with the feeling of missing her eyes on me. Leave it to the asshole who gave me life, to ruin the most extraordinary moment of mine.

Chapter 32

L eslie Anne

    I study my daughter and the Alphas son who are sitting across from me on the small couch in his father's office. For someone who looks an awful lot like the intimidating man sitting before us all, he certainly does not act like him at all. The way my daughter and he share a connection is fascinating. If I'm being honest with myself, I'm past jealous, as I watch them from my seat.

I move a moment, trying to get comfortable in this tiny chair, and instantly regret it. My ribs are broken, since I'm not a werewolf or witch, I'm not officially a part of them. So, according to Bartholomew's laws of his pack I must heal on my own. I want to do nothing more than to give him one of the nastiest looks I can fathom, but I'm too cowardly. After all, I'm the only human in the room.

Judging by the dangerous smile I can see from my periphery that is now placed on the Alpha's face, he knows exactly what I'm thinking, and loves my fear. I'm certain everyone here in the room can smell it pouring off of me in waves. When my daughter clears her throat, I use all the strength I have left, forcing myself to lift my head to look at her.

"Leslie, you have a lot to explain." The sound of my first name falling from her lips breaks my heart.

Ever since she learned to talk, I have always been mama or mother. Never once has she dared to call me by my name. Licking my dry, cracked lips, I do my best to clear what feels like cobwebs from my throat.

To my utter shock, Ezekiel stands from the couch, walking past his father, who is now glaring at his only son and pours some water into a small paper cup, his father has here in his office. When he walks it over to me, I have to hold back the tears that want nothing more than to fall from my eyes. It's nothing really, in the perspective of most people, however with how I have been treated here as of late its one of the kindest gestures I've had towards me these last few weeks.

As though I am nothing but dirt below everyone's shoes. How do they look away or simply walk in the other direction when they see Arthur treat me poorly out in public. I know most nights they can all hear my screams and cries as he takes me roughly, and against my will, but as I've said before I am not a true part of their world. Therefore, no one can help me, or heaven forbid do the least nice thing and speak kind words for me at all.

"Thank you." I whisper to him as I put the cup into my wrapped-up hand.

I'm certain it is broken, as Arthur didn't appreciate the dinner, I made for us two nights ago and stomped on it as my punishment. All he did was throw bandages at me, telling me to wrap it up. So, I did the best I could. I hold back the wince, as I bring the cold liquid to my lips, and drink it down in one gulp.

Once I'm finished, he goes so far as to take it from me, throw it away, and walk back to sit with my daughter. I take in a deep shuddering breath, holding it in for a moment, before letting it out. Trying my best to calm my racing heart.

"What would you like to know darling?"

I keep looking down at my hands. I can't bring myself to look into her eyes again. Not right now. Not knowing she's so disappointed in me for so many reasons.

"Please look at me."

The sound of her voice has a lone tear falling from my eyes. Chastising myself, as I promised, no matter what I wouldn't allow myself to be upset when I saw her. Slowly, ever so slowly, I bring my face up to look into her gorgeous sky-blue eyes. When she was little, I used to tell her I could almost see clouds within them they were so light. It would make her giggle and smile wide at me. Causing my heart to feel as though it had grown with her happiness.

She isn't looking at me with happiness right now. All I can see is devastation, sadness, and confusion. I want to look away so badly, but in a way, I feel like I owe her this.

"Tell me everything." She demands.

I bring my good hand to my hair, brushing it behind my ear with my fingers. A nervous habit I've had since childhood.

"Okay, well..." I sigh out loud.

Trying to think back to that night. Where this all began really.

"I was six weeks pregnant, with a guy's child I barely knew. It was one of those friend of a friend scenarios and we were at a party drinking." I say with a shrug of my shoulders. As though that makes up for my poor behavior.

"I was excited, and I made it very clear to him that I wanted nothing from him. I would raise the child all on my own."

She looks at me with furrowed brows, but before she can utter a word, I hold my hand up to her. Letting her know silently that I'm getting to the part where she comes into my story.

"Everyone that I worked with, and that played a part in my life was excited for me. I was over the moon with joy." A small laugh falls from my mouth with the memory of just how happy I had been.

"I was working a double shift one night, and on my way home I felt a sharp pain in my lower stomach. I didn't know what was going on, but I thought it was nothing, so I continued on my journey. Only the pain grew worse, and I could feel something wet rolling down my legs." I know my eyes are glazed over as I recall the most horrid night of my life.

"Placing my hand down there, I was scared to bring it back up. Knowing full well what I would see." I lick my dry lips, as I close my eyes.

I don't want my daughter to see how much this memory truly affects me.

"Sure enough, there was blood there. I spent that night crying my eyes out. Screaming and hollering profanities at God. Feeling torn apart with what he had done to me." Opening my eyes, I look right at my girl.

Giving her a sad smile, I continue on, "I even took that weekend off. Telling everyone my morning sickness was horrible."

"I decided I didn't want everyone to know what had happened, so I faked my entire pregnancy. I stuffed my shirts with a belly I bought off the internet and did what I could to be convincing. I never thought about what would happen when the baby was supposed to be born." Wiping my nose with my sleeve, I take another deep breath. Trying to gain my composure so I can discuss the rest of it.

"As luck would have it, I didn't need to worry about that." I give the sincerest smile of my life to my daughter.

"It was a winter night, and I was going for a walk to get some fresh air. It was the first night of my maternity leave from work, and everyone was expecting to see my new baby within a week."

"I was trying to come up with how to tell everyone what had happened when it began to rain. Well, more like freezing rain, as it was the dead of winter."

"I hid in a crevice I found between the fire department and one of the old, crumpled buildings for a little shelter. Figured I'd wait it out, and then the most extraordinary thing happened. I heard a man and woman's voice a few feet away." I maneuver my position in the chair trying to get more comfortable.

"I had to squint my eyes to see what was in the woman's arms. Then, I saw a little baby, that she was holding close to her bosom. She was saying something about how she didn't want to do this, that she couldn't leave you there. However, the man was practically shaking her entire body with his hands on her arms. Telling her it was the only way."

Pausing a moment, I reminisce inside of my memories. The face of the woman, so similar to that of my daughters. Only the woman's held nothing but sadness then.

"I watched, in the pitch black as she kissed you repeatedly. The man kissed your forehead, and they left you in a basket, bundled up. To keep you dry from the storm and warm from the cold. Knowing someone would find you soon. They were correct. Only it wasn't a fireman." I look up at my daughter. Holding her gaze, wanting her to know I mean every word I'm about to say.

"It was me. I came out of my hiding place once they had gone and picked you up from that basket. Looking down at the most precious little human I have ever seen in my life. I saw knitted into your blanket was your name. Bethanna Delaney. I thought it was beautiful, but just in case if they came looking for you later on, I changed it with the same letters of course." Shrugging my shoulders at her, I wipe away the tears that I allow to fall freely. As they are a sign of happiness.

"You became my little Annabeth. I raised you as my own, and I don't regret one second of that." My words come out with conviction.

I may have made some mistakes in my life, raising her as my own will never be one of them. She was a baby with a need for a family, and I was a woman in need of a child. We both got what we needed that night.

Chapter 33

Annabeth

     I sit here, holding onto Ezekiel for dear life. How my life came about is astonishing to me.

"What could their reasoning be for leaving me there?" I whisper more to myself than anyone else in the room.

Going over and over the information my 'mother' just shared with me. I want to say that I'm certain they had a good reason, but I don't know if that is the truth or not. Seeing as we have no idea who they are I may never know.

"I'm not certain, only that the man who is your biological father was very adamant on the subject. The only other words he had said to your birth mother was this was for your own good, to protect you."

At that word my head pops up to look at her, my eyes growing wide. Releasing my hold on Ezekiel, I stand from the couch, and walk behind it. So, I have room to pace.

I move from one side of the room to the other, completely ignoring anyone else in the room. Thinking of the story over and over in my head. It's my way of processing everything.

"Well, your parents did always have a flare for the dramatic." At his voice my pacing comes to a halt, and I turn to face the devilish Alpha, who sits upon his thrown in the room.

He sits there looking bored, his chin along the back of his hand, and looking at me with a tilt to his head.

"That's right. You knew my parent's." At those words, my feet move at their own accord.

Not stopping until there is a mere foot between the Alpha and myself. I can feel the tension radiating from Ezekiel's body, as he stands up from the chair and walks his way to stand behind me.

134

"That I did. However, we weren't close per say. I know very few things of them." He lifts a brow at me while speaking those words.

Something in my gut tells me he's lying. I can see it in his eyes. Opening my mouth, I go to call him out on it, when the feel of Zeek's hands pull me back, until I hit the front of his body.

"I know what you want to do, but I'm asking you not to right now." He whispers in my ear.

Causing the boredom that was once placed in his father's eyes to disappear. A look of unadulterated excitement fills his eyes. He sits a little straighter, coming to the edge of his seat. His hands falling between his slightly spread legs.

If I didn't know any better, I would think he wants me to cause a scene. That he's expecting it and waiting for a good time to strike. What he will do to me if I open my mouth and allow the words to be free, I haven't a clue, but the fact that Zeek is begging me to not do it tells me everything I need to know.

Lifting my chin, I evade his stare, turning to my mother and giving her a sad smile. "Thank you for telling me the truth Leslie."

Without another word to her or the Alpha of the pack, I walk from the room. The sound of my footsteps echoing behind me as I make my way to the front door. Without a care right now, I open it up and make my way down the extravagant steps that align the front of the mansion.

I can feel the tears welling in my eyes, but I do my best to hold them back. No one here deserves to see my weakness. As I'm about to reach out for the handle of Zeeks car, I hear the distinct sound of gravel below someone's feet from behind me. A hand beats me to the handle and opens the door for me. I don't have to look to know it's Ezekiel. I knew he would follow me. Knowing full and well that he would want to be here for me.

Without a word I sit my ass on his leather seat of the passenger side of his vehicle. Closing my eyes, I try to fight the tears from falling, as I hear the door close from beside me. I can almost see in my mind's eye, him walking around the front of his car and opening his door. Once he is seated, I hear the distinct sound of the keys turning in the ignition, and the vehicle purring awake.

The feel of his body close to mine, has my eyes opening. He reaches over, grabs the seatbelt and clicks it into place. With a hand on my chin, he rubs my cheek with his thumb, before kissing my forehead. Once he's all settled, he pulls out of the long driveway, making his way to the front gate. Ignoring the guards, that clearly want Zeek to roll down his window to talk, he speeds forward, the tires squealing behind us.

Normally, something like this would cause me to freeze up, and hold on tightly to the handle, but my body feels nothing right now. I am completely numb. Knowing I need a moment, I lay my head back and close my eyes to get a little rest. Once we make it back to school, I know he'll wake me up, and we will have to talk about how I'm feeling. Until then, I only enjoy the sound of the engine purring as we drive down the road.

Ezekiel

I didn't want to show my hand in the presence of my father, but when I seen the look in her eyes, and watched her mouth open I knew she was going to say something rude. Well, in his eyes that is rude. I couldn't allow that to happen, knowing full well what he would do next. I have seen too many people crumble under his cruelty.

After everything she just found out, I couldn't keep quiet while he did everything in his power to bring her further down. Meaning the war that is brewing between my father, his men and mine would come to an abrupt head today. I don't have the right resources yet for that.

Luckily, she must have sensed how much I truly meant by my words. She simply closed her mouth and walked away. My father growling at her back. I had to hold back the laughter that was bubbling up at the expression on his face. Quickly bowing my head to him, I ran after her, once I caught up, I did what I could to get us out of there fast.

Not that it really matters, I know a battle is going to be pursued here shortly. Once we get back to school, the boys will have all her things in my dormitory, meaning I am her new roommate. That thought causes a sinister smile on my lips. She doesn't fully understand what's happening between the two of us, but I have been raised in this world.

Probably thinking she's just a play toy for me right now. Once I have her, I'll grow bored and walk away. Little does she know I'll never tire or bore of her. She was born into this world as mine. She has no choice, and once I have her below me, screaming my name and begging me for more. Then, I can complete our coupling with a bite, and make her mine for good.

The moment we come together, mating for life, I know I will have more power than my father could ever dream of. She and I will take down the destitute families that run the board in our world. Being the only true mates alive right now in this world will make us the new king and queen. We will finally be able to rid this life of the monsters who created it, and change things for the better.

All thoughts come to a halt once I'm parked in my spot. Turning the keys, I look over at my extraordinary and beautiful mate. She fell fast to sleep, not surprising as the busy and emotional day she had.

Feeling eyes on me, I pull mine from her beautiful face, seeing Roman with his arms folded over his chest, he nods his chin at me. Letting me know he and the others are finished. All her things are in our room now, he moved into the dormitory with Leo and Deluca. Meaning I'll have her all to myself tonight.

Chapter 34

A<u>nnabeth</u>
    I'm not certain how long I've slept for, only that when I stretch my arms over my head, I hit a headboard.

"Ow..." Bringing my hand to my chest I hold it within the other.

. My eyes are still closed, so without another thought I stretch my hand out and feel what I'm laying on. Certainly, enough its bedding. Comfortable sheets and a comforter at that. With the feel of those below my fingertips my eyes pop open, and I look around the room I am now in with a daze.

The last thing I remember is being in Zeek's car, driving back to school. After finding out all the information from Leslie about my real parents. A laugh coming from the corner of the room has me sitting up and turning my head in that direction. My mouth waters at the sight before me. Ezekiel sits in the chair he has in the corner, only he's wearing nothing but a pair of tight boxers.

I can see his manhood is hard and very ready. My tongue falls from my mouth, licking my lips with anticipation. My thighs tighten with want. My breasts ache for his touch. *What is happening to me?*

At the sight of his sinister smile, I know immediately he can read my thoughts all over my face. He sets his glass down along the side table, I was so distracted by his body I hadn't realized he was drinking anything. With the smile plastered on his gorgeous face, I watch as he slowly stands from the chair. The movement causing his muscles along his chest and arms to flex.

I bring the light blanket that is covering my body closer to my neck. Tightening it so much I'm practically trying to use it as a shield. I must swallow down my need for this man with every step he takes closer to me, as I lay on his bed as though I'm a sacrifice for him. He stops all movement tilting his head to the side.

I cannot see too much in the darkness of the room, but I can imagine that brow of his lifting up in question.

"You really believe that blanket is going to save you from me?" His voice comes out playful, as though he finds me amusing. He takes a step closer, and I immediately try to move to the other side of the bed.

I'm not certain why, there's perspiration forming on the palm of my hands, my heart rate is beating a hundred miles a minute, and my body feels as though it's on fire.

"I know it won't, but for some reason I feel the need to use everything I can to put some sort of space between the two of us." I tell him honestly.

The humorless laughter that falls from his mouth the second later, has my blood boiling.

"What's so funny Ezekiel?" The use of his full name brings fire to his eyes.

"Oh baby, we are going to have so much fun tonight." His words are cryptic.

I know if I told him no, he wouldn't push me, he's not that way. I also know it will be incredibly difficult for me to say that. For unknown reasons I want this man more than I have ever wanted anyone in my life. He brings out the animal that lives inside of me. Both figuratively and I suppose literally with who my parents are.

Let him touch us... the sound of a voice coming from inside my head has me freezing where I am. *We need him to touch us, we'll feel so much better. Trust me.* My thighs tighten at the thought, as I rub them together trying to give myself the pressure I desperately need.

With the idea that I'm hearing voices, I feel as though I'm falling crazy. "Who said that?" My voice comes out as barely a whisper. I'm not even certain Zeek heard them.

He pauses just by the bedside. Close enough to touch me, but instead he looks around the room. His brows pinched in question.

"Who said what?" All the cockiness has slid away from his face, as he takes the opportunity to sit on the edge of his bed.

I bite my lip in contemplation on whether I should mention to him about the female voice.

"There was what sounded like a female voice talking in my head." My shoulders fold into themselves, as I look down at my hands along my lap.

When I dropped the blanket away from body I haven't a clue. My thumbs rub together with trepidation and fear. I'm afraid I may be losing my mind, and I'm feeling antsy knowing he is going to touch me so much more than he already has tonight.

"What did she say to you?" At his calming voice my head shoots up, and I make direct eye contact with him for the first time since I woke up.

Swallowing the nervousness, I'm clearly feeling, I bring my hand up and play with my hair. Twisting it around my finger, as I explain to him what I just heard.

He studies me for a moment, before a sincere full-blown smile forms along his lips. He's showing me his pearly whites, and I have to say I love this smile on his face almost more than his devilish and sinister one. Almost!

"She's finally waking up beautiful." He tells me as he brings his hand up to my cheek.

Rubbing the backs of his fingers along my skin. I quickly drop my hand back to my lap, hearing it land on my thigh, but I pay it no mind. All my focus is a hundred percent on the delicious man sitting before me.

"Who is?" I asked him quietly. Already knowing the answer and fearing hearing it for the first time.

He doesn't answer me right away. Simply scoots closer to me on the bed, bunching up the blanket with one hand as he tightens his hold on my face with the other.

"Your wolf baby girl." I feel his breath along my lips as he speaks each word. Just like that my life is forever changed with four little words.

"You mean to tell me that I'm like you?" I know it's a stupid question.

Clearly, I am, as I come from another powerful wolf family. However, living in the human world, and only hearing about werewolves in stories is making this a little hard to believe.

Instead of answering me, his eyes focus on my lips. Bringing his thumb to my bottom one, he rubs it back and forth, causing me to whimper. I want to touch him more than anything in this moment, but I'm afraid to take this next step with him. Not knowing what it will mean, or what will happen if I do.

He bends his head, so his face is right up in front of mine. His lips are touching my lips, as he tells me "You know you are."

He gives me a peck on the lips before pulling back. That devilish smile that I've grown to love and become familiar with is back on his face.

"You know what else baby girl?" He coos.

I swallow, trying to get the dryness of my throat clear.

"What?" I ask fearing his answer.

Without meaning to I eat up the little space between the two of us. Our lips are once more a hair breath away from one another.

"You're not only like me, but you're my fated mate."

With those words something happens to me. I don't know what, but with the wideness of his eyes and the shock plastered on his beautiful face I would say it's something incredibly important.

Chapter 35

E<u>zekiel</u>
    I was hard before she woke up, sitting in my chair thinking about all the things I was going to do with her once she opened those gorgeous eyes of her. Now that I know her wolf is waking up from the lifetime slumber, my cock is like granite. My hand reaches out to touch her face. I'm intrigued with the beauty of the yellowish green eyes looking back at me.

"She's waking up baby girl." I whisper so close to her lips our breaths mingle.

Her brows furrow in confusion, and I smile brightly.

"Your wolf is looking back at me right along with you." She backs away an inch from me, her eyes growing wide in surprise.

"That, it can't be, I mean..." Her voice breaks off as she tries to turn her head away from me.

I don't allow that. I want her eyes on me the entire time. I rub the silent tears that are now falling down her cheek with my thumb. Her response breaks my heart to pieces.

"I know you were hoping it was truly a mistake, and perhaps you wouldn't have to think about it after today. As you can see, it's not a lie baby girl. You're just like me." I whisper my words, with a breathy tone, as I bend that much closer to her lips.

My tongue licks both our lips, causing hers to open with an intake of breath. One that conveys need and want just as much as I'm feeling.

I can't hold myself back any longer, I attack her with everything I have. We are nothing but tongue, teeth, and hands. Mine feeling every part of her body I can get them on, hers digging into my hair. When she moans, my mouth swallows the noise right up. I have been spending all this time watching her sleep. Taking a brief moment to talk to Roman about how things went with moving her things.

He told me it wasn't too much of a problem as her roommate just spoke up once asking if he was certain. All he had to do was look at her, and she coward. Apparently, she took off to her room, and shut the door. Once all her things were here, I called the office to let the principal's secretary know what was happening that day.

He wanted to holler at me, tell me I am not allowed to live with a female student. Once he took the phone from her ears, he growled at me, thinking that would frighten me. I think he may have forgotten who was on the other end. Once I growled back, I could picture his tail falling between his legs, as he tried to hold his bladder.

I mentioned to him who she was to me, and that was the end of the discussion. He mumbled something along the lines of "Whatever I felt is best," and he hung up the phone.

Leaving me laughing in the wake of the phone call. Now, here I am, Annabeth living with me, without her knowledge right now, and kissing the hell out of her.

She tries to pull away, but the beast is already half unleashed. I pull her hair, telling her I'm not close to being through with her yet. Feeling her nails dig into the skin on my shoulders, has me panting beneath my breath, as I pull away from her. Apparently, at some point I bit her lip. There's a little blood from the small cut on her lip near the corner. When I lick my lips, my eyes practically roll back in my head from the euphoria her blood brings alive on my taste buds.

A growl works its way up my throat. *I need more.* With that thought I open my eyes and stare her down. I can see the movement of her throat as she swallows down worry. I know how she's feeling. I can smell the fear and want wafting in the air of the room.

"You have no idea the things I plan to do to you tonight." My voice comes out in a carnal tone, as I lick my canines.

Her breathing has picked up. Her chest lifting and falling with the effort it's taking her to breath. Tilting my head to the side, I give her a devious smile.

"What's wrong baby?" I purr the words.

Causing the throb of her heart in her throat to beat a mile a minute. I bite my bottom lip as I imagine the taste of her skin and blood filling my mouth when I finally claim her there. Her thighs move, as she tries to get the friction her wanton pussy desperately needs.

"Take the shirt off." With those words, her eyes lift to mine once more.

I can see the gears moving behind her eyes. She's wondering if she should do this. Follow my direction and do as I say without a fight. I know from the look in her eyes staring back at me that she wants nothing more than to fight me. The real question is will she want to win over her stubbornness?

Knowing it may take her a moment, I stand from the bed, not releasing her eyes from mine. I step back, until I feel the chair hit the back of my legs. Once I know I've reached my destination, I sit back down. Lifting one leg over the other knee, I steeple my fingers, placing them below my chin. Nodding toward her, telling her she has a certain amount of time to do as I say.

When she looks around the room, anywhere but at me, that just will not do.

"Annabeth..." My voice comes out breathier than I expected.

Causing her to look right at me.

"Do as I tell you, or I'll get up from this chair and do it for you."

My words ring true, only if I move from this chair, I'll do more than take off her shirt. She must know my thoughts without me speaking to them, because her hands go to the bottom of her shirt. Just before she lifts it up, I can see her once again doubting her actions.

"I won't do anything without your permission, but I can see by the way your body responds to me, and the look in your eyes that you want this just as much as I do."

She doesn't deny my words, only looks down at her lap.
"Tsk, tsk, tsk..." I bring a finger up and shake it.
"None of that now baby." At my words she looks up at me once more.

Biting her bottom lip, she causes my body to squirm as my cock grows that much harder with my need for her. I know she's not trying to be seductive, but the truth is my little vixen doesn't need to try. She is the single most sexiest woman I have ever laid my eyes on, and I fully intend to burry myself deep inside that delectable body of hers tonight.

Chapter 36

<u>nnabeth</u>

A   Am I really going to do this? Allow this God of a man to take me tonight? Hell yes!! My inner wolf shouts at me. Causing all my willpower to go out the window. Within the next moment my shirt is clear over my head, and I'm throwing it on the floor. Not paying attention to where it lands. My eyes are squarely on Ezekiel, waiting for his next demand.

He tries with all his might not to smile; I can see by the way he looks down at his lap for a moment. He's trying to gain his composure, understanding fully that I will stand from this bed and put my shirt back on.

"Now the pants." Although his voice came out as a whisper, the meaning behind them causes me to jump.

"I...I'm not sure..." I stammer along, trying to form the right words with what I'm thinking.

"You don't have a choice. Remember?" His words ring true.

When I look up at him, I see he's sitting forward now. His elbows on top of his knees. His hands dangling between his spread legs. My eyes must have a mind of their own, as they follow his pecs all the way down his stomach. To the little line of hair, leading me right to what I want to see the most.

Once I get a good look at the bulge in his jeans, I lick my lips with the sudden desire that has swooshed through my blood stream. *I want that in every hole of our body.* Shaking my head, I can feel my cheeks turning a beat red with embarrassment. I cannot believe my wolf just thought that.

Calm down girl. I haven't even had anything in my most important one, let alone every hold within my body. I chastise her.

Oh, believe me. I know we will enjoy it immensely. She practically purrs inside my head.

The sound of Ezekiel's sexy laugh brings me back to the now. When I look up, I see his head tilted to the side, as he studies me with the precision of a hunter.

"I can only imagine what your wolf has just said to you lamb."

I bite my bottom lip, as his look upon his face turns smoldering.

"Don't get me wrong I can imagine it was very dirty." The last word comes out of his mouth in a growl.

"I can already tell that her and I will be having so much fun together."

Looking down at my hands, I ask the question that has been bothering me since she and I woke up.

"Would you rather be with her all the time over me?" My voice comes out softly. So low, that if he wasn't a werewolf, I know he wouldn't have heard me.

"Lamb, look at me." He speaks just as softly to me.

I want to, really, I do, but I can't bring myself to do it. Instead, I continue looking down at my intertwined hands. When I hear him stand abruptly from the chair, my eyes close so I can't see him once he reaches the bed. As he sits down beside me, I don't have to worry about that, as he brings his hand below my chin and lifts my face to his.

"Annabeth, open those glorious eyes of yours and look at me." His words come out so sweetly. I can't fight him any longer.

They open, and a second later I feel the tears begin to fall. He observes my face deeply with his own eyes. I feel his thumbs wipe away the falling droplets on my cheeks.

I watch as he releases my chin with one hand, to bring that thumb to his lips. I observe closely, as he sucks the digit into his mouth, making a show of licking my essence from his skin.

"I want you on me now." I don't even recognize my own voice.

"We will get to that." He whispers.

"First, let me tell you here and now that I want you. I crave you." He holds my chin roughly between two fingers.

Looking deep into my eyes he tells me, "I have been obsessed with you long before I knew who you really were. The first moment I saw you I was a goner." His words cause my heart to erupt with pure joy.

"Do you understand Little Lamb?" That eyebrow of his lifts up once more, causing me to smile.

Nodding my head, I let him know I heard every word he spoke. Showing through my eyes just how much they mean to me.

He bends down so close to my face; I can feel his breath on my lips. "Take off those pants of yours baby girl, and then you can have me."
Within the next second, my hands are undoing my button and pulling my zipper down. Without breaking eye contact, I pull the material down to my knees. Kicking them off a minute later.

Biting my lips, I tilt my head at him. In a snarky tone, I ask him "You going to stand there all night, or will you take what's yours?" Lifting a brow at him I'm practically daring him to make the next move.

There is a moment of nothing but complete stillness and quiet. I swallow down the sudden feeling of embarrassment. I lay before him, as a sacrificial lamb, with nothing but my see-through, black panties and bra. The need to cover myself is strong, but I will not allow anything to ruin this moment.
Finally, after what feels like hours of him deliberating, while looking at my body from the top of my head to my toes. His hands reach for his boxer briefs.

Slowly, ever so slowly he pulls them down his thighs. I watch mesmerized as he pulls them all the way down his legs and kicks them off his feet.

His penis is so hard and long, the length reaches his belly button. I can't control the gasp that falls from my mouth.

"Will that thing even fit inside of my innocent body?" I don't mean to sound frightened, but with the look of that thing I can't help for my tone to come out that way.

I must have been scooting up the bed, farther away from him without even realizing. Because he reaches for my ankle and pulls me back down the comforter. Once my legs are over the side, his body crashes down on top of me.

The next second his mouth is on mine, tongue fighting for dominance inside my mouth. It must have done what was needed. As my mind goes completely blink, with nothing but the feel of desire coursing through my body. The need inside of me is so strong I'm afraid it may burst out of me.

Chapter 37

E zekiel
       I have to make sure I take this slow, although my wolf wants to do the complete opposite. I'm fighting both him and me at this moment. All I want to do to my woman is ravish the hell out of her.

"Please Zeek I need you inside of me." She whispers along my lips.

Her begging causes me to have a sinister smile, as my mouth moves down her chin to her neck. The sound of her growl actually has me laughing at her antics. I suck her pulse rate on her neck, making her squirm her hips. She's now fighting to get closer to me.

"What's wrong baby girl? I breath upon the skin of her neck.

"You're torturing me. It's not very nice." She whines.

When I laugh my breath falls upon her skin, causing goosebumps to form on her neck and down her chest. I kiss all the way down, licking between her breasts, and bringing my hands to them. Cupping them with both and massaging them in circles.

The fact I can see each pebble of the skin on her nipple causes my wolf to come to the forefront. Opening my mouth, I place the entirety of her nipple in my mouth, nibbling it through her see through black bra.

"Oh, you are killing me with this thing." I speak with a growly tone.

"Do you know how much I have to fight myself. So, I do not rip this bra and panties away and devour your body." The truth falls from my lips.

"Please do." Her words come out breathy and low.

With those two words, the thin thread that was keeping my beast held back is gone. The next moment, I'm placed in the back seat of my mind, as my wolf takes over. We sit up, our knees on both sides of her hips.

With both hands, we rip apart her panties, lifting her hips and dragging it the material from below her body. I throw it behind us without another thought. My mouth waters with the smell of her honey reaching my nose. I lick my lips at the sight of her pussy lips drenching the comforter below her.

Needing to get my mouth on her, I lift my hand in front of her eyes, watching my claws grow. Her breathing picks up, as her eyes open wider. The scent of both her want and fear causes a sardonic laugh to fall from my mouth.

"Scared baby?" I ask, my voice sounding entirely too animalistic.

When she nods her head yes, it makes me excited for what's ahead. Slowly, I bring my index claw to her bra, right at the thin material between her breasts. My eyes make their way up her body, as I eat her up with both. I pause on those plump, beautiful lips of hers, before making my way up to her eyes.

I know she's feeling a little afraid, not knowing how to handle my wolf right now. This is all known to her, that of course will change as time goes on. I can also see the trust shining back at me within her eyes. The fact that she can work her mind through that fear that she's feeling, knowing I will not hurt her at all, brings nothing but pure joy to my heart.

I show her just what it means to me, looking at her with a smoldering look. She smirks at me, her breathing calming at the sight of the look staring back at her. She spreads her legs further apart, almost daring me to take her now. With that little devilish movement on her part, I flick my wrist and cut the material in half.

Without another pause, I rip the material clear from her body and throw it behind me. Climbing between her legs, I spread them further apart so I can fit my entire upper body between her legs. Then, I attack her mound with everything I have.

Annabeth

The things he's doing to my body is almost magical. He's burying his tongue straight into my pussy, as he rubs my clit continuously with his thumb. Then, he switches it up just as fast, as he licks up to my clit, sucking and biting it with his teeth, as he pushes three fingers directly into my vagina.

I can't hold myself back, my hips raise from the bed, as I bury my hands in his hair. I don't know what's happening to me, but I feel like I'm watching this all unfold from somewhere in my mind. As though I'm no longer in control of my extremities.

He lifts his face from between my legs, taking a hold of both my hands with just his one and slamming them above my head. I briefly saw strands of his hair rip clear from his scalp. It doesn't seem to phase him though, If anything it only excites him all the more.

"Now I have both of your attention." He purrs the words along my lips. Causing me to open for his onslaught. His three fingers are still doing their magic with my pussy. When he does a come-hither motion with two of them my head falls back along the pillow as a scream fall from my mouth.

A devious laugh falls from his lips. "How about one more little lamb?" I know it's a rhetorical question.

He's not expecting me to answer him, just to simply take what he's giving me like the whore I have clearly become. He pumps all four fingers repeatedly, in a consistent motion, causing my muscles to convulse. I'm almost there, my orgasm right on the cusp of igniting when he pulls his fingers clear from my body. Causing me to whimper out loud.

"What I have coming next is going to be so much better baby girl." He says as I feel something hard and powerful at the entrance of my pussy lips.

He waits for me to open my eyes and for them to fall into his, as he plunges my more than ready body for the first time.

Chapter 38

E **zekiel**
      Wow, being inside of my woman feels amazing! Nothing has ever felt this divine, and I've had my fair share of women. Hell, I've had a lot of men's share of women. I look down at her as my body freezes entirely. I'm both checking her face for any signs of discomfort, and soaking this moment in. It's nothing I've ever experienced before.

My eyes practically roll in the back of my head from the euphoria. Bending my face closer to hers, I go in for a chaste kiss, but she grabs hold of my head and goes in full speed ahead. She bites my bottom lip with her teeth, causing me to open up for her.

"More! Oh, fuck me please..." She moans into my mouth.

Sticking my tongue inside I swallow up her words, making them mine forever. With those five little words I lose all sense of control. Pulling my hips back, I plow forward, over and over again.

Her hands leave my head, making their way to my back. I feel her claws grow longer, as she rips into my skin. My lips leave hers, as my head falls backwards on a growl.

"Marking me little lamb?" I ask her sardonically as I look deep into her eyes.

"You love it." Her voice comes out more animalistic, her eyes are a golden color.

Meaning her wolf is at the forefront. I let out a laugh, as I pick up my speed with how fast I'm fucking this delectable body of hers.

"You know I do baby." I lick her lips with my tongue.

The sound of her screams is music to my ears. Lifting my upper body, I piston my hips repeatedly into her. I can tell from the look on her face she's close to coming. Bringing my hand down between our bodies, I roll circles on her clit with my fingers, her claws digging into my back sticking there.

153

"Fuck!" I holler aloud.

A moment later, I feel the bones in my hands changing, as my own claws grow. They rip into the comforter beside her head, as she lets out a scream to the top of her lungs. Her pussy engulfs my cock, as her body spasms repeatedly with the orgasm wracking through her body.

Annabeth

Holy shit I have never felt anything like this before. My wolf is howling inside of my head, as I scream at the top of my lungs. The sound of it echoing off the walls of the room. I cannot believe we are doing this together. It feels so right, like I never want him to stop.

"That felt fucking incredible, but I'm not finished with you yet." His words purr in my ear, as he sucks it into his mouth.

The next moment, as though I weigh nothing at all, he flips my body over, and places me on all fours. The pillow that was once below my head, he now places below my hips. Lifting my lower body up more for better access for his cock.

I don't have any time to ask what he's doing, as he plows back into my ready body. In this position, I feel much more full of him. His chest falls to my back, as one of his hands is placed on the back of my head. He pushes it down to the mattress, so my cheek is laying along the comforter.

Then I feel both his hands along my hips, as he rams into me from behind repeatedly. The power I feel from him with each movement of his hips is mind blowing. He's taking me like an animal. All I can do is bunch the comforter with my hands, holding on for dear life.

"Do you know how crazy you make me? How often I have pictured doing just this to you the short amount of time I have known you?" He asks with every thrust of his hips.

I know these questions are rhetorical. As there is no way I can answer him with everything I'm feeling and the things he's doing to my body. The only coherent words falling from my lips are 'yes' and 'more'.

I feel his hand wrap around my throat the next second, as he lifts me clear up and my back slams against his chest. He holds it there, tightening a little. Not enough where I cannot breath, only enough so I can feel the power of his dominance.

"Do you know the first thing I thought the moment I saw you lamb?" He slows his movements allowing me to shake my head no at him.

I fell his lips move into a sadistic smile along the skin of my neck. Just before he licks the pressure point there. Within the next moment I feel his teeth nibble the area. Causing the muscles inside of my sopping pussy to spasm around his cock.

A demonic laugh falls from his mouth, "Just one more second baby."

I don't know the meaning of his words, but I feel his other hand work its way between my legs. He knocks my own hand away and rolls little circles around my nub with his own fingers. Causing my hips to jerk with the feeling shooting through my body.

"I thought I'll make that woman mine." He whispers along my neck.

I'm about to finish just as I feel his hard cock kick and the first squirts of his semen inside my unprotected body.

"That moment is now." Those are the last of his words I hear before he sinks his teeth into the skin of my neck, causing me to holler out in both pain and pleasure.

My second orgasm of the night coursing through my body. Before my vision grows blurry and I fall to the bed. The room turning black.

Chapter 39

A nnabeth
It takes me a moment for my eyes to open, my vision to focus once more. Seeing what's around me, I can see I'm still in Ezekiel's bed. Stretching my arms at my side, a sharp pain shoots within my neck, spreading throughout my body.

"Ow, what the..." My words pause as I bring my hand to the bandage there.

"I told you, "The sound of his voice breaks into my thoughts.

Looking to the side, I see him sitting in the corner of the room, in that same chair of his. Legs spread out, one hand bent at the elbow, his thumb playing with his bottom lip. Head tilted to the side, as he studies me. The other hand laying along the arm of the chair, with a drink of bourbon in a small glass in his hand.

My hand reaches for my neck, feeling a bandage there. My brows furrow in confusion. I give him a mean look, that only makes him smile devilishly. My wolf is happy, I can feel her emotions. The woman that I am not so much.

"What did you do?" My voice comes out in a low warning tone.

It doesn't scare him in the least. No if anything it causes him to look bored with me. He sighs animatedly, before rising from the chair. He downs the little bit of golden liquor in his glass, slamming it against the table.

"I told you." He looks over at me, a predator look held deep in his eyes. Causing my heart to stutter.

"I was making you mine before the night ended." He shrugs his shoulders. Lifting his head, he looks at the clock on the wall. "You've been asleep the last two hours. Passed right out." His eyes cut to me once more. A predator smile forming on his lips. The smile so bright I can see his teeth in the dark.

Licking his canine, he walks slowly closer to the bed. I want to cower in his presence when he's like this. Instead, I lift my shoulders and stare at him head

156

on. Once he reaches the side of the bed, his body so close to me he can reach out and touch me, he stands there looking down at me.

Observing me like the wolf he is. At his most delectable prey.

"It's just a little past one in the morning. Meaning I kept my word." His hand lifts to my chin, rubbing my bottom lip with his thumb.

"How did you make me yours exactly?" He watches the movement of my throat as I swallow down my fear.

Deep in my heart I know how he did it, but I want to hear the words come from his mouth. How he took advantage of me in a weak moment. Sunk his teeth so far into my skin I know there will be a mark there always.

He bends his head, so his face is right in front of mine. Goose bumps form along my skin, as my heart rate speeds up with his close proximity. There's nothing more I wish to do than to pull him down and attack him like the wanton slut I've become.

"I bit the area on your neck just before you shoulder." His words come out as a matter of fact.

I feel appalled at his actions, or should I say how he went about it. I make a move to look down at my hands along the comforter. Wanting to look away from his eyes so badly. He doesn't allow it. Yanking on my hair so hard, a pain shoots through my scalp.

"No, no Lamb. Look at me when we talk remember?" His eyes look between mine. I can see a look of determination held deep within his.

I decide in this moment, fuck it all to hell! He wants me to look at him, fine I will. I'll give him a piece of my mind while we are at it.

Ezekiel

The look in her eyes has made me harder in moments. I know she's about to tell me exactly what she is feeling right now. The wolf and man part of me cannot wait to hear it. Only the animal part of me takes over the moment she opens her mouth.

I bend my face even closer, diving my tongue into her open mouth. I think she's going to push me away, instead to my delight she reaches both hands into my hair and pulls me closer to her body. We both fight for dominance. Our tongue doing the same dance we have had since first meeting.

I know she's using this to her advantage. Punishing me with her body instead of yelling her feelings. She pulls the short strands of my hair, before reaching behind me and clawing her nails into my back. I know there will be blood and marks there later on. It shouldn't but the sadistic part of me loves this.

I growl into her mouth, as she takes the noise and swallows it down her throat. The next moment, there is a sharp pain and I taste my blood in my mouth. She pulls my bottom lip in her mouth, sucking my red essence into her mouth.

When she pulls away, she has some of my blood dripping from her lips. With one hand she wipes it away with her thumb, then placing it into her mouth and sucking it from her skin. All the while never breaking eye contact with me.

My hands have reached for her before I realize what I'm doing. Only, she jumps out of the way, clear off the side of the bed, her hands at her sides rolled into fists. Knowing this is going to take a while, I sigh and lay my body straight out. Bringing my hands behind my head, giving her my full attention.

Chapter 40

Annabeth

How dare he look at me as though he wants to devour me! If anything, I'm more pissed at my own body and mind. I want nothing more than for him to do all the dirty things I can see playing out behind his eyes. He lifts one eyebrow at me, looking at my entire naked body. Not leaving one crevice left without a prowl.

"Got something to say Little Lamb?" He makes a show of his hand going to his chin, as he looks up at the ceiling. "Or should I call you, my mate?" His voice is condescending.

That's it, he's done it now. Looking around the room, I find my jeans and shirt ripped to shreds. So, knowing I need to cover my body, before I leave here, I gather the sheet that is half off the bed. Luckily, his body weight isn't holding it down.

Without giving him any more attention, I wrap it around my body like a toga, tying a knot at the top. Making sure it's tightly done, and I won't have to worry about it falling at my feet, giving everyone a visual once I'm in the hallways and outside.

"Cat got your tongue?" At his question my eyes raise to his. I glower at him, not giving him the satisfaction of answering any of his questions.

Instead, I walk to the door. I hear his movement along the comforter on top of the bed, as he growls at my back. "I wouldn't try to go out of this room in nothing but my sheet. It could be deadly." At his words I pause with my hand on the doorknob.

"Are you threatening me?" I look at him out of the corner of my eye.

He shakes his head at me, "I would never harm you in any way Lamb, but I can't hold back what I may do to anyone else outside of this dormitory." Turning around I study him thoroughly.

I can see he means exactly what he says. Placing one hand on my hip, I give him my full attention. I half expect him to lay back, getting comfortable and looking smug. He does none of that, instead standing from his bed and making his way to me.

Once he's close enough to touch me, he moves so fast I didn't even see it coming. He places his hands around my hips, grabbing a handful of my ass and lifting me clear from the floor. Slamming me against the door I was trying to escape from moments ago.

Our faces are so close to one another, our noses are touching. I can feel his breath along my lips. He looks almost angry, as he breaths heavily. "You have always been mine, and you may not like how I went about it, but I did what had to be done. For both of our sanity."

I look between his eyes, only seeing the truth looking back at me. I open my mouth to ask what he's talking about when there's a sound of the door to the dorm opening and slamming shut. He places a finger to his lips, as we hear the foot falls of someone in the room. A moment later, there's a knock at the door at my back.

"What the fuck do you want Roman. We are busy." At the name of his best friend, my shoulders relax a bit.

"I can smell that, but you may want to take this call." At Romans words we look at one another confused.

"Go into the bathroom and clean up Lamb. I'll see what this is about." He releases my legs from his hips and sets my feet onto the ground. I go to walk away from him, but he pulls me back and kisses the hell out of my lips. Making me dizzy.

When I finally walk a few steps away from him he slaps my ass. He watches me the entire way to the bathroom, blowing me a little kiss as I close the door. I lean my head against the door, catching my breath. This has been one hell of a night.

With that thought I wonder who would be trying to reach him at this hour. Cracking the door open a smidge I watch as he takes the phone from Roman's hand and talks to whoever is on the other end of the line.

When he says the words, "You spotted her parents? Are you sure?"
My ears perk up.

Someone spotted my biological family. They are still alive. I open the door completely, gaining both the men's attention. However, the only one I'm looking at is Ezekiel. He doesn't break eye contact with me, as he hangs up the phone and hands it back to his friend.

"Leave." His voice is so low it's scary.

I don't pay attention to Roman at all. I only know he does as Ezekiel tells him because I hear the door shut quietly to the dormitory. Leaving me alone with the young man who has confused me since the day I met him. The one who makes me feel alive and wanton like no one has ever been able to do. The man I trust the most in this world.

"Tell me."

Milton Keynes UK
Ingram Content Group UK Ltd.
UKHW040653140923
428670UK00001B/130